BY: K'VONNE

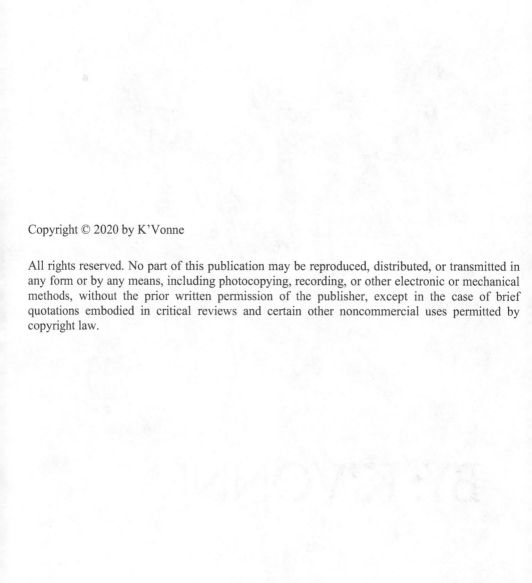

Bone swiveled around at the sound of Rayne's piercing scream. His eyes zeroed in on Kiana lying on the ground. The color of her white wedding dress changing to crimson red. She has been hit in the chest. Bone took off in a sprint running over to Kiana and collapsed on his knees beside her.

Rayne stood there sobbing and shaking uncontrollably as Bone hollered, "Someone call an Ambulance." He caressed Kiana's head from the ground placing it in his lap. Bone whispered to her attempting to keep her alert. Mason had been hit as well. Everyone attending the wedding frantically ran around like chickens with their heads cut off. Still concentrating on Kiana, Bone continued shouting out for someone to call for help. Finally, he heard the sirens in the distance. By then, he noticed her struggling to breath. Bone uttered, "Please please hold on!" Help was on the way.

Kiana was attempting to tell Bone something. But he shook his head ignoring what she tried to say. Concerned, Bone was afraid that Kiana was tired of fighting. She was starting to spit up blood. Bone knew that's never a good sign.

"WHERE THE HELL ARE THEY? He bellowed looking around the crowd. Tears were rolling down his cheeks as he feared they wouldn't make it in time. "URRRGGGHHHH! " He belted out. Looking down at her he could see that she was scared. "Hold on baby, Bailey needs you. I need you." He whimpered, resting his head on her shoulder.

The EMT'S arrived yelling for everyone to clear the way. They finally recognized those in need of assistance. Bone allowed, when a couple rushed over to help Kiana. The other responders went to work on Mason. Bella was crying and standing right by his side. She hopped in the Ambulance following the stretcher on which Mason was placed.

They had to work on Kiana some before they put her on the gurney. She was drifting in and out of consciousness. Bone stayed right there as they worked on her. She was his wife and he was going to be there for her. The medics were running back and forth trying to assist with both wound victims.

When one of them yelled out they lost her, Bone damn near fell to the ground. They rushed her to the Ambulance and began using the Defibrillator. Her heart started beating again and they shut the doors. Bone hurried up and jumped on the Harley he'd brought to ride off on. He followed behind them all the way to the hospital.

The sirens were loud and disturbing to say the least. They were a good fifteen minutes away from the closest hospital. On the ride Bone noticed a car following closely behind him. He knew that could possibly be the fuck nigga responsible. As he slowed down some trying to look back.

The car slammed on the breaks and backed up. He tried watching it as they turned around in the middle of the road. If he could see the tag numbers, but he couldn't see a damn number. He wanted to chase the car, but he had to get to the hospital. When he arrived, he parked his bike and quickly ran inside.

He asked the receptionist question after question. She didn't have anything to tell him though. They hadn't even checked her in or anything yet. After he calmed down some he strolled into the waiting room. Rayne and Bella were sitting in there, eye balling each other.

When Rayne saw Bone, she jumped up and ran over to him. She embraced him in a tight hug. She was worried about Mason and her sister. And she knew that he was as well. He hugged her back, but he wasn't there to comfort anyone.

He just hoped that his wife would pull through. An hour later the doctor came out and announced that she didn't make it. Rayne immediately broke down. Bone just froze up at the words she didn't make it. This wasn't supposed to be the end…not yet.

He couldn't believe that she was gone. They were supposed to be heading to Jamaica in an hour. And now she's gone just like that. Bone couldn't believe the turn of events that had taken place. How could he find the woman of his dreams, and she be taken away from him so quickly?

They were just married ready to start their lives together. Making more babies were what he thought would be next. Living to be old with grand and great grandchildren. Not one of them dying the day of their wedding. How could the best day of his life turn into the worst day of his life?

All he knew was somebody had to pay. And they were going to pay with their life. Kiana's life was taken, but it surely won't be the only one.

Mason was laying in the hospital bed. Bella had been by his side the whole time he'd been in there. His mother had visited, but he didn't want Shantel seeing him like that. He hadn't seen Bone since the wedding. He totally understood with everything that he's going through.

He thought about Rayne almost every day. Mason wanted to call her up several times. But Bella was always around he never had a minute to himself. She was finally going home to shower and change. He was glad because he was going to call and check on Rayne.

Bella walked in her parent's house. She was wanting to get in and get right back out. But they had saw the news the night of the wedding. And she hadn't been home since that night. Magnus and Angela were hardcore Christians.

They wanted their daughter to marry a man out the church. Her parents thought she was still a virgin. What little did they know, Bella gave her goods up a long time ago. She was sixteen when she gave it up to her first love. Angela called her in the living room.

Her father wanted to have a very long talk with her. She went sulking in the room and took a seat. She already knew why they were calling her in there. They wanted her to stop wasting her life. All Bella wanted to do was have fun and enjoy life.

But they didn't want that for their only child. Lord and behold they find out she's dating a drug dealer. All hell would break loose. Her mother would pull out the oil while her father reads the bible. So, that was something she had to keep a secret.

"Bella, we know that you were at that wedding that had the shooting. Our friend was there, and he said that he saw you. I didn't want to believe that it was you. But when he showed me a picture of you hanging all over a thug." Shaking his head, he just starred her in the eyes.

He didn't want to contemplate his baby girl out in the world being a floozie. She wasn't raised that way. Bella was brought up in the church. Angela had always saw the whore tendencies in her child. She knew that she had got it honest.

Before she became a heavy Christian, she was worldly. She was out in the streets in her younger day. She was trying to prevent her daughter from making the same mistakes. Magnus couldn't stomach his baby girl being worldly. He was brought up in a family that went to church every Sunday.

His sister's all married men from the church. And that's what he expected Bella to do. She hadn't been staying home and he didn't like it. He went to talking to her about the bible. She sat there and listened until she couldn't take it anymore.

Bella stood up she didn't want to hear all that. She came home to shower and change clothes. Holding her hand up stopping her father's rant. She politely told her parents that she was eighteen years old. She was grown and didn't have to live by their rules anymore.

"Young lady the day you stop going by the rules of this house, must be the day you move out." He retorted getting upset.

Standing there Bella looked back and forth between her mom and dad. She could tell that he was serious.

"Fine...I will leave." She muttered storming off to her room.

"Bella no...Magnus tell her not to leave." Angela begged her husband.

He held his hand up and went back to reading his bible. She went after her daughter. Angela didn't want her to move out the house. She tried talking her out of packing up her things. But Bella wasn't trying to hear anything she was talking about.

She packed up enough of her things to get by for a while. After she went out the door Magnus looked out the window. She got in a car and drove off without a care in the world. He knew she was in the guy's car that she was at that wedding with. His fear was confirmed that day...his only daughter was worldly. Praying for her and putting it in the lord's hands was all he could do.

Back at the hospital Mason tried getting in touch with Rayne. She wasn't answering her phone. He was worried about her and his boy Bone. He was getting out the next day in time for Kiana's funeral. Bone was putting her away in queen status.

The next day Bella drove him home. When they got inside she had to help him get dressed. He wanted everyone to wear all black. Kiana was going to be in all white in an all-white casket. He was also having eighteen white doves released in her honor.

Bone was decked out in his all black suit. He was in mourning and he looked like it to. His ass was in a different frame of mind. Finding the person responsible for killing his wife was his top priority. But first he had to send his lady off in style.

Riding his motorcycle to the church. He hopped off and strolled inside. His mother and sisters were seated up front. She never got to meet her son's wife. The plan was to have a family dinner, when they came home from their honeymoon.

But with the turn of events, it was never gonna happen. Bone walked down the aisle to the front of the church. When Bone stepped up he didn't see the casket. It was a damn Urn sitting on the mantle. He pulled the preacher to the side and asked where his wife's body was.

He told Bone that she was delivered that way. He couldn't believe that Kiana was cremated. After the services the hospital had some explaining to do. He let the preacher get to his job. Bone was pissed off and he was ready for some answers…from everybody.

The pastor performed the services. And he did a wonderful job sending Kiana off. Bone couldn't wait for all of this to end. He hated funerals and especially this one. When it was over they released the doves.

He kissed his baby then turned and asked his mom to watch her for him. She said she would, and she would get Kiana's remains for him as well. Bone then hopped on his bike and sped off. His thoughts were all over the place. Kiana being cremated might not have been such a terrible thing.

Bone didn't know why the hospital did that shit. But he thought about it, she would always be with him. He decided to let that shit ride. He wasn't about to let the motherfuckers that killed her get away with it. She wouldn't be in that Urn if it wasn't for them assholes.

He first stopped and grabbed a bottle of, liquor. He had to get his mind right. Life without Kiana wasn't what he wanted. He didn't desire to stay on this earth. But Bailey needed one of her parent's around.

He was drinking and riding around. Bone needed to find someone who knew something. He knew that he had to keep his ears to the streets. Pulling up at the trap he got off and marched inside. He motioned for a few of their workers to come outside.

Bone offered twenty -five g's to the person that get him some information. The four guys took him up on his offer. They decided to work together and split the money. He didn't care what they did. He just wanted the person responsible for his wife's murder.

He hung around a little while longer. Finishing off his bottle, he dapped the rest of the crew up. He was heading home for the night. Hopping on his bike he sped off. As he rode down the road, her saw the ABC store was still open.

Bone pulled in and parked his bike and got off. He marched inside and picked up a fifth this time. Bone wanted to stop the thoughts running through his mind. He figured if he could stop the thoughts of Kiana, the pain would go away. He paid and strolled out the door.

He got back on his bike and popped the top on that bottle. He took a nice long swig before getting back on the road. He staggered inside his house and plopped down on the couch. Bone sat there drinking and crying. He wouldn't show his true feelings in front of everybody.

Shit he didn't like showing his true feelings period. Sitting there crying he felt like a whole bitch nigga. He didn't believe that men should cry. But losing Kiana the way that he did, he couldn't stop the tears. So, he drank as much as he could before he passed out.

Chapter 3

Rayne was stressing out over the fact that her sister was gone. And not to mention that Bella bitch being at the hospital. She felt like her ass had some nerve being there. She couldn't help but to feel sorry for herself. Who was going to be there for her now?

Mason had moved on with that light skinned bitch. And Kiana was gone. She didn't have anybody now. She sat back on the sofa and cried. Rayne cried for her sister and herself.

Mason had been calling her phone. But she wasn't talking to him right then. He had his new bitch on his arm. Why was he calling her is what she wanted to know? She heard her son in the other room crying.

That broke her from her train of thought. Wiping her tears, she got up and went to check on her boy. She waltzed in his room and saw him standing in his crib. He was getting big Malik would be one on Saturday. And she wanted to do something special for him.

She wanted to have a small birthday party for him. But Shabazz was still taking all her money. So, now it had to be something that didn't take money. Lifting him up out the crib, she carried him to the living room. Rayne sat him down on the floor with some of his toys.

His little ass was content for a while. She grabbed the pipe and lit it up. Shit she had to have something take the edge off. She took a couple pulls doing just enough to get right. Rayne kept looking at her phone.

She wanted to call Mason back so bad. But she just couldn't do it. Her pride and her ego wouldn't let her. Shabazz came roaming in all wild eyed and shit. Something was off with his ass.

He had been tripping and very secretive lately. He went straight to the bedroom and called her to come in there. She didn't feel like being bothered with his ass. His ass knew that she was mourning the loss of her sister. But he didn't give a fuck about that.

She got up and moped to the bedroom. Malik went crawling right behind her. When she got to the door she saw him lying on the bed. His ass had stripped butt naked jacking on his dick. Rayne knew what time it was, and she knew that she didn't have a choice.

"What do you want Shabazz?" She asked looking down at Malik pulling on her pants leg.

"Girl what do you think I want? Come suck on this dick." He quipped moving his hand up and down his shaft.

"The baby is right here and he's hungry." She remarked hoping he would leave her alone.

"Just leave him there and come over here." He stated starring at her.

Rayne knew that he would throw a tantrum if she didn't. She went to pick Malik up, but Shabazz yelled at her. And said to leave him right where he was. She wanted to take him back to his room. How was she going to suck dick with her baby in the room?

She knew he wasn't old enough to know what she was doing. But she still didn't want to do it. Slowly make her way over to him. She climbed up on the bed and took his dick in her hand. Rayne couldn't help but to look over at her son.

She took his dick inside her mouth and went to work. Because that's what it was. It wasn't something she wanted to do at the time. He was making her perform this act. Shabazz could tell that she wasn't into it.

Her ass wasn't making him feel good. Opening his eyes, he looked down at her. Her eyes were trained on Malik instead of handling her fucking business. Getting ticked off he punched her in the back of her head. Rayne didn't see the blow coming as she went flying back.

She was hearing birds chirping in her head. The pain was excruciating as she held her head crying. She had no idea what she did wrong. Hell, she was doing what he asked.

"YOU'RE ONE STUPID BITCH!" He shouted standing up off the bed.

"Wha…what I do?" Rayne stuttered crying.

He picked his pants up off the floor. Rummaging in his pocket he pulled a needle out. It was already pre -filled with a drug. He had planned to use it later himself. But since Rayne was being a stupid bitch, he was gonna share the greatness with her ass.

He pulled his belt out his pants. When she saw what he was doing, she hopped up off the bed. She thought he was getting ready to beat her ass. Little does she knows that's the last thing on Shabazz mind. He stalked up to her while she cried and pleaded. Grabbing her by the arm he wrapped the belt around it snug.

"What are you doing Shabazz? I'm sorry for whatever I did wrong." She assured him backing up against the wall.

Rayne cried as she watched him prepping the needle. She had never used a needle to get high before. He tightened the belt on her arm. When he found a good vein, he injected the liquid in her bloodstream. Her eyes went to rolling in the back of her head.

She was on a whole new level. Cocaine and crack rock didn't have shit on it. Shabazz smiled as she slid down the wall. He knew her ass was gone for a minute. Picking up his son he got him a bottle and put him to bed.

He was ready to go catch up with Rayne. That Heroin was the damn devil. But he loved the way it made his ass feel. Going in the room he took the belt and needle then hooked himself up. The next morning Rayne woke up still sitting on the floor.

Looking around the room she saw Shabazz laid out on the bed. Forcing herself off the floor she went to the bathroom. Handling her business, she hurried to go check on her son. He was laying in his bed drinking on his bottle from the night before. Picking him up she took the old bottle.

He didn't want to let it go. She made him a fresh bottle and changed his diaper. By that time his punk ass daddy strolled through. He had on his boxers and nothing else. She despised him now and she planned to get away from him.

She watched him drinking milk out the gallon. Now he knew damn well that was Malik's milk. Rayne had enough, she had to leave. When he went back to bed she heard his ass snoring. Getting off the couch she picked her son up and snuck out the door.

Walking down the street she went to the closes store. Going inside she asked to use the phone. She called up Mason and asked him to come get her. Thinking about it Rayne knew she didn't have any family. She was all alone in this big ole world.

Mason pulled up and she got in the car. He noticed the lump on her head. But he didn't say anything about it. He drove her to his house. He knew this was getting ready to be crazy.

Bella was living with him now. And he didn't mention anything to neither woman. They got out and roamed inside his apartment. Stepping in his place Rayne could feel that something was different. She knew that she wasn't going to like it either.

"BABY IS THAT YOU?" Bella hollered out from the back.

"YEAH IT'S ME." He shouted looking at Rayne. Mason could see the uneasiness in her eyes.

Bella came out the room in some green girl boxer shorts. With a black tank top without a bra on. Her nipples were on display for the world to see. She had a bright smile on her face. But when her eyes landed on Rayne, it was obvious she wasn't happy to see her.

She had a disgusted look on her face. Mason knew it was gonna be some shit. Having his current girl and his baby mama shacked up in the same crib. Yes, he was dating Bella, but Rayne was his heart. And he would always be there for her regardless who he with.

"Why is she here?" She asked with a look as if she was constipated on her face.

"Because she needed somewhere to lay low for a while." He retorted waving his hand for her to go on with the bullshit.

He told Rayne to sit down and make herself comfortable. She did as she was told. Bella huffed and stormed out the room. Shaking his head, he went right behind her. Rayne sat there listening to them argue back and forth.

She couldn't believe that Mason had moved that bitch in. His ass was really moving on with his life. She didn't quite know how to feel about it. It was an hour later when he emerged from the bedroom. She noticed that it got quiet in the room.

Rayne figured they were in there having sex. She felt sick to her stomach just thinking about it. When he came out he wasn't fully dressed. Picking up Malik off the couch and her bag. She was leaving, her feelings were deeply hurt.

How was he gonna fuck that bitch while she was there? Then to make matters worse. He sat down on the couch laying his head back. Looking like he was all relaxed and shit. Standing up she headed towards the door.

"Where are you going Rayne?" He questioned sitting up.

"AWAY FROM HERE." She shouted breaking out in tears.

Mason jumped up off the couch. She was walking down the street. He saw her then he ran after her. When he caught up to her he turned her around. He couldn't just let her leave with nowhere to go.

"Why are you leaving? He inquired seeing the tears running down her face. Rayne, come back in the house. Please."

She didn't want to leave. Hell, she didn't have anywhere to go. But she knew that her and Bella living together wouldn't workout. He kept starring at her, waiting on her to say something. When she didn't respond he held his hand out for her bag.

They marched back to his place and went inside. Bella was watching them from the window. Why did he go chasing after her ass? She couldn't figure out what kind of hold Rayne had on him. When they got close to the apartment she backed away.

She thought about leaving. But she refused to let Rayne win. Sitting down on the bed she went to thinking of a way to get her ass out of there. Mason knew fucking Bella with his baby mama in the living room was wrong. That was the only way to get her to shut up.

He got Shantel's room ready for Rayne and Malik. She hadn't said one word to him since he came out the room. He figured she knew what went down in his bedroom. Hell, he had two women in his house at the same time. Bella moved in on her damn own.

Mason didn't ask her to move in. But she was there and Rayne, well she will have to get over it. He retired to his bedroom drained. Shower, then off to bed in that order was his plan. When he stepped in the room Bella was sitting up waiting on him.

Her arms were folded across her chest. Attitude was written all over her face.

"How long is she gonna be here?" She quizzed watching him looking through his drawer.

"Long as she needs to. Look I'm not gonna argue with you about this. She's here either deal with it or…" He started but she cut him off.

"Or what Mason?" She questioned with pride laced in her voice.

Rolling his eyes in the back of his head. He didn't feel like going through the bullshit.

Shabazz woke up later that evening. Getting out the bed he went to the kitchen for a beer. Coming out he noticed the house was very quiet. Scanning around he didn't see Rayne or Malik. Putting his beer down on the table, he went to look in his son's room.

He searched every room in the house. They weren't nowhere to be found. Looking outside all around the house and neighborhood, he even asked Mrs. Shirley. And after she threatened to shoot his ass, he found himself back home. Snatching his beer off the counter, he marched back into the living room.

Sitting down on the couch he opened his drink and took a big ole swig. He thought that maybe she took Malik for a walk. But as the daylight turned dark, Shabazz knew her ass had ran off. He couldn't believe that she took his damn son. Jumping up off the couch he stormed into the bedroom.

Getting dressed he snorted the last of the coke. He was officially out of everything. He had a good high going, but he knew it wouldn't last. He knew he was a bold mother fucker. Because he was going to one of Mason's spots to get some dope.

When he pulled up he peeped Bone sitting on the stoop. Look like that clown was drinking on some liquor. And Shabazz wasn't that fucking bold to walk up on his ass. So, he sat there watching him grieve. He could tell he was in turmoil.

He thought it was funny that he caused his ass some pain. The same way that he'd caused him pain for a week. So, he made sure that Bone's pain lasted a hell of a lot longer. Since there altercation he wasn't about to risk getting his ass beat again. While he was waiting on Bone to leave, Mason drove up.

Scooting down so he wouldn't see him. Shabazz peeped over the dashboard watching him as he strolled inside. He sat back and waited on him to come out. Mason wasn't in the trap long. He ran back out hopped in his car and peeled out.

Pulling out behind him he made sure to stay several cars behind. He had some pay back for his punk ass to. Mason never noticed he was being followed. He pulled up at home and went inside. Shabazz was two apartments down.

Now he knew where he rested his head. And that was a major plus in his book. Shabazz was parked outside of his apartment for two hours. That taste for his high started getting the best of him. He had to make a move and get right.

Mason roamed inside and went straight to Rayne's room. He told her she had to do that shit outside. She was a little pissed off. His ass didn't make her go outside before. She knew he was making her now because of Bella.

Rayne wanted to argue with him about it. But she didn't have the energy for it. She got off the bed and stormed out the room. Mason looked at her and shook his head. He didn't know how he was gonna live with two women at the same time.

He didn't want to make Rayne mad. He just didn't want Bella all up in her business. She didn't need to know that she smoked crack. And he was going to get it for her. Her uppity ass would defiantly have something to say.

And he didn't have time for the petty drama. He took care of Malik until she made it back in.

Meanwhile Shabazz was feeling great and on his way to Mason's. His ass sat and watched the apartment for days. The day he same Rayne walk out the door, changed his whole demeanor. He wanted to confront her ass. But if she screamed that would alert Mason's ass.

He didn't want him to know that he knew where he lived. So, he sat back fuming. She had him fucked up. Running back to that bitch nigga. He couldn't wait for the opportunity to talk to her ass.

His ass cased the joint day after day. Mason left a few days later. And once again Shabazz followed him undetected. He got out at the store where he worked at. Waiting for 30 minutes he knew that he must've clocked in.

Rushing back to the apartment, he got out and marched to the door. Turning the doorknob to his surprise it was unlocked. Going inside he could hear Rayne and Malik. He heard another TV in the back. That made him think that Mason would be back soon.

Quickly making his way to the room he heard Malik, laughing and giggling. He rushed inside and startled her. She wasn't expecting to see Shabazz coming through the door. She hurried up and picked up her son. She didn't know what he was there to do to her. Fear filled her heart as she starred into his eyes.

"What are you doing here Shabazz? How did you find me?" She quizzed holding her son tight.

"Don't worry about that…get your shit and let's go." He retorted stepping up closer to her. he wouldn't hesitate to snatch her ass up if need be.

"No, I'm not going with you." She muttered afraid of what he might do to her.

"Oh, your ass is going with me. I don't know who the fuck you think you're talking to. Bitch I will fuckin kill your ass right now." He emphasized grabbing her by the arm. He wasn't about to play games with her ass.

"OKAY!" She shouted hoping Bella would come help her.

"Don't try it bitch…I will kill you and whoever else is in this bitch. You know what…fuck your shit. Let's go now." He chided pulling her by the arm. Shabazz didn't want to kill anybody today. All he wanted was his family. But he would take whoever out that tried to intervene.

Rayne got just went with him. She didn't like Bella's ass, but she didn't want anything to happen to her. He dragged her by the arm all the way to the car. A couple times she almost dropped Malik. But she held on even tighter to him.

When he pushed her inside the car he slipped up running his mouth. He told her he should kill her like he killed her sister. His ass was so high and pissed that he didn't realize what he said. But she heard him loud and clear. When he got in and drove off she turned and looked at him.

"Did you just say that you killed Kiana?" She questioned with tears laced in her eyes.

"Bitch what the fuck are you talking about?" He inquired. He wasn't about to admit to committing murder.

"You said that you should kill me like you did my sister." She confirmed wiping the single tear that slid from her eye.

"BITCH SHUT THE FUCK UP AND WORRY ABOUT THIS ASS WHOOPING YOU GONNA GET WHEN WE GET HOME!" He belted getting pissed off that he fucked up.

She sat there crying, Rayne couldn't believe that he killed her sister. She knew that he was crazy. But not to the extent to kill someone. He had threatened her on several occasions. And she never really thought that he would do it.

But now she wasn't so sure that he wouldn't follow through with it. All kinds of questions ran through her mind. She couldn't figure out how he found her. He didn't know where Mason lived. Or so she thought anyway.

Chapter 4

Bella heard Rayne talking to somebody. But she wasn't concerned with her ass. She wanted her to get out of there. Getting dressed she was going hanging out with her home girls. She was tired of sitting around the house.

Listening to somebody else's baby cry. That shit was for the birds. After she finished getting herself together she strolled out the room. The front door was wide ass open. She looked around the living room for signs of Rayne.

She didn't see her anywhere. She looked around the house and outside. Bella couldn't figure out where she had gotten to. Her and the babies, things were still in the bedroom. Something wasn't right so, she called Mason to let him know.

He told her that he was on the way home. The shit just wasn't adding up. She sat and waited on him to get there. When he showed up he didn't even say hey or anything. And that shit made her feel some type of way.

"What happened Bella? Where could she be?" He was running around like he was bound to find her.

She just sat back and watched him getting tee'd off. Why is he so worried about her ass? This shit was beginning to be too much. Bella didn't know how much longer she could take this shit. She wanted things to work with Mason.

But all his ass seemed to be worried about was Rayne. She could admit that it was crazy for her to leave her things. He called up Bone telling him about Rayne. He was going to pick him up and they were going looking for her. Pissed off Bella left right after he did to hang with her girls.

Bone was sick and tired of people fucking with them. He was to the point where he was gonna shoot first ask questions later. Too many mother fuckers got to slid nowadays. When Mason scooped him up he got in loading his piece. He saw the way his boy turned and looked at him. But he didn't give a fuck.

They rode around looking for her. Even went by Shabazz's house. There was no sign of her anywhere. Hell, they didn't even run across his corn ball ass. They did see some of Shawn's people.

Bone wanted to jump out on their asses, but Mason said they didn't need the beef. They didn't know who had killed Kiana. Nobody ever came with any information. There were just some speculation and that's about it. Bone truly believed that it had something to do with Shawn.

Dropping him off at the trap, Mason drove home. He was pissed and worried about Rayne. it was something different about her leaving this time. Normally she would take her things. But this time she left everything including her purse.

When he arrived at home he waltzed inside. He just knew that Bella was gonna be running her damn mouth. But to his surprise her ass wasn't even there. Mason was happy about that. He showered and laid down for the night.

All kinds of thoughts raced through Bone's mind. He knew he had to get some get back on them nigga's. they caused his girl to have his baby early. And then they killed her. How could he let that shit ride? It wasn't gonna happen.

Bone hopped on his bike after Mason drove off. He was gonna get some damn answers from Shawn's men. Speeding past them as they strolled down the street. When they heard the roar from his bike, they took off running. He chased they down the street.

He was certain one of them knew something. And Bone was going to find out. Picking up speed he zoomed right past them. Slowing down he stopped swinging his bike sideways. He pulled out his gat and aimed it at them. They stopped running and held their hands up in surrender.

"Whoa whoa dawg, what's this all about?" One of the younger dudes questioned.

Bone didn't say shit. He got off his bike keeping his eyes trained on them. If they didn't give him some information. They wouldn't make it home.

"MOTHERFUCKER TELL ME WHO KILLED MY WIFE!" He belted at the one that had something to say. But his ass wasn't saying what the fuck Bone wanted to hear.

"Yo man we haven't killed anybody." The other guy blurted scared for his life.

"WHO KILLED HER THEN? BECAUSE SOMEONE THOUGHT IT WAS A GOOD IDEA TO PULL A FUCKING SNIPER MOVE AT MY DAMN WEDDING!" He bellowed looking from one dude to the other.

"I swear on my children, we didn't have anything to do with it." The first guy said.

"Oh, you swear on your children huh, well this is for my daughter who doesn't have her mother anymore." Bone muttered letting off a shot to his dome. Then pointed the gun to the other guy before the body hit the ground.

"OH SHIT! MAN, I SWEAR I DON'T KNOW ANYTHING ABOUT A SNIPER AT YOUR WEDDING! PLEASE DON'T KILL ME, PLEASE!" The boy begged.

"So, you still don't know shit?" He inquired already knowing the answer.

"NO MAN I SWEAR I DON'T KNOW ANYTHING ABOUT IT!" He confirmed hoping that Bone believed him and let him live.

"Well in that case." He concluded letting off a shot to the boy's chest.

The body dropped but he wasn't dead. Bone stood there standing over him. He stood there and watched the guy suffer just like Kiana did. It didn't surprise him one bit that he got satisfaction from it. Shawn and his clan better watch out. Because he was just now getting started.

Shawn was chilling on his sofa watching basketball game. When he heard a knock on the door; he grabbed his 45 on the coffee table. Normally he didn't have visitors. And if he did they have guest at his house. If he did, they knew to call first.

Creeping to the door he peeped through the peep hole. He saw Tahiti standing his porch. He wondered why she was there. Opening the door, he moved so, she could come in. Shawn could tell that she was upset about something.

"Shawn tell me now did you have anything to do with that shooting?" Tahiti asked pacing back and forth.

"Woman what shooting are you talking about?" He asked sitting down.

"The one at Bone and Kiana's wedding." She stated watching him.

He sat up wondering where she got that crazy ass idea from.

"Tahiti what are you talking about?" He asked getting up off the couch. Shawn had no clue as to what her ass was speaking on.

"Don't play stupid! I know you had something to do with the shit. That's probably why you took me out of town." She retorted placing her hand on her hip.

"Look Tahiti I don't even know what you're talking about. So, stop accusing me of shit I don't know about." He warned getting tee'd off.

She stood there second guessing herself. Maybe he didn't know anything about it. Her aunt Rita called her yelling in the phone. Talking a bunch of smack about her baby daddy. She was all riled up which caused Tahiti to get that way.

"Well my aunt called me talking about you shot Mason and this and that." She revealed hating she assumed that Rita was right.

"And instead of asking me, you came in here saying I had something to do with the shit." He addressed rubbing on his head.

"I know I shouldn't have come at you like that, but…" She protested before Shawn cut her off.

"But nothing…you should've asked me and not accused me." He quipped just as his cellphone rang. Bending down he picked it up and answered it.

"Yo, what's going on?" He asked into the caller.

Tahiti could tell it was serious by the tone of his voice. He went to the back of his crib. She could still hear him talking. When he came from his room he told her he had to bounce. His emotions were all over the place.

Here he was at home watching the game chilling. First his baby mama come over flapping her damn gums. Then he received a phone call about two of his men getting killed. Shawn was the type of businessman, he tried to avoid drama. But when you came for him, you should damn well expect him to come back.

She didn't want him to leave before they finished their conversation. But she knew she shouldn't push her luck. They were in a good place right now. And she loved being back with her son's dad. When Rita called her with that bullshit, she thought she would have to leave him alone.

Before he left he asked her where Josiah was. She told him that a neighbor was watching him. Shawn didn't know what was going on. But he wasn't going to risk something happening to his family. He told her to go get Josiah and get back to his crib.

Tahiti asked him why and what was going on. But he didn't have time to explain. He told her to grab some clothes for them both. They had to stay with him for a while. She didn't really have a problem with it.

She just knew that she wouldn't be able to have clients there. They left his house and she went her way and Shawn went his. Arriving home, she did as she was told. She made sure to grab her appointment book. Tahiti got her son and went back over his house to stay.

Shawn meet up with his workers after talking to his main man Ant. No one saw what happen to the young workers. So, he told everyone to watch their family members closely. He wasn't trying to bury anybody else. He put some workers on the street and told the guys with family to go home.

After the meeting Ant had a problem with losing money. They were trying to make up the huge loss they took. But Shawn wasn't worried about that right now. He just wanted some answers and all his men to be safe. When they finished talking he called Tahiti, making sure they were alright.

When she said that they were at his crib. He knew that they should be alright. His ass was stressing over everything that was happening all at once. He needed a drink so, him and Ant went to the strip club.

Chapter 6

Shabazz pulled up at home and parked. He told Rayne that she better not get out the car.

He got out and marched around the car. She saw the look in his eyes as he made his way around

to her door. He opened it and grabbed her by the arm.

While he was sitting in the living room feenin, Snow called his phone. He answered, and

they talked about a few things. He missed his best friend. And them falling out over some drugs

was stupid and petty. He was coming over and bringing some blow.

It's wasn't his drug of choice. But beggars can't be choosers. When he arrived, they

talked and got high like old times. Rayne could hear them in the other room. When she heard

Snow's voice she hoped he didn't mention that she sucked his dick.

If he did she knew that Shabazz would beat, her ass again. She strolled into the living

room. She wanted to get high to. It had been days since she had any drug. She just hoped that

Shabazz let her get a taste.

When Snow saw Rayne come from the back, he got all giddy inside. He didn't know that

she was back with Shabazz no good ass. Why didn't he meet her first? Is what he always thought

in the back of his head. She sashayed into the living room wanting to get high.

She knew she was looking a hot ass mess. Her natural hair wasn't twisted. She was just

rocking a nappy afro. She had been meaning to call Tahiti to do her hair. But being back with

Shabazz she knew that wasn't going to happen.

Shit was getting crazy around the way. Since Mitch got murdered the drugs was drying up. He never introduced Mason or Bone to his connect. They were meeting up at one of his traps. They were gonna have to come up with a way to get more supply.

Sitting in Mason's car they were discussing the situation. When a strange car pulled up and stopped. Bone grabbed him gun ready to bust. He wasn't feeling somebody rolling up on them. As the window descended he lifted his gun and aimed.

"Whoa young buck I come in peace." Dave stated grinning at the young hustlers.

"Man, who are you and what do you want?" Bone quizzed still holding his piece up.

"I don't want anything young buck. I heard y'all were looking for a connect. And I have everything you could think of. Here… he handed a card out the window. Mason took the card and looked over it. Meet me at that address in an hour if you're interested."

Dave told his driver to pull off. Bone could finally relax. He had heard of Dave. The streets talked, and word was he had that flame. They talked it over and they were going to meet up with him.

Shit they needed that come up. They were now their own boss and had four traps to maintain. On the way Bone had him stop by the ABC store. Mason noticed that he had been drinking a lot more these days. He knew his best friend was in pain.

But he was going about it all wrong. He still had his daughter to think about. And he should be pouring all his love onto her. Bone sipped on his drink while they rode to the spot. When they arrived, it was an old abandon building off in the cut.

They were both strapped just in case some foul shit popped off. Hell, they knew this could be a set up. But they were determined to get a connect. Getting out the car they marched to the door. Before they could knock the driver opened the door.

He patted them down checking for weapons. He took their guns and allowed them inside. They were both a little hesitant about it all. But when they were led to a different part of the building, their eyes lit up. Dave wasn't lying when he said he had everything.

There were bricks and bricks all over the room. Pills were in baggies in stacks of boxes. And guns were hanging all around the walls. He was into a little bit of everything. Shit, Bone was in aww with the stuff he had.

He was down for selling some guns. That was right along his alley. Dave came out the back happy to see them. He had heard wonderful things about the duo. And when he heard through the grapevine they were in need of a connect, he had to reach out.

He was all about making money. And the young guys seemed to be the same way. So, he knew they were meant to work together. Strolling into the room he waved them over to a table. They sat down and got right to it.

"I'm happy to see that you guys came to talk business." He smiled at them.

"Yeah well we need supply and from the looks of things…you got what we need." Mason quipped looking around the room.

"Indeed, I do…so let's get down to it then." He replied feeling good about doing business with them.

They talked about how much they wanted up front. When they established that then it was about the numbers. It took some time for them to agree on that part. But they arrived at a reasonable price. He had men there to place everything in his trunk.

As they did that he told them that he was available 24/7. His cellphone number was on the back of the card. But once they used that number he would give them a new one. He never used the same phone number twice. He finished up with them got up and roamed out the room.

Bone sat there thinking that the old head was a weird one. They got up and bounced. Mason wasn't comfortable with riding around with all the dope in the car. Neither of them was totally sold on Dave just yet. Hell, this could all be a set up.

They watched the rearview mirrors, the whole way back. They just knew a cop was going to pull them. But that didn't happen. Heading straight to the trap they cooked up the coke. They were back in business and was looking to make a lot of money.

It took them all night to get everything ready. Going from trap to trap setting the workers up with work. Every one of them were happy to be back making money. Bone took over two of the traps leaving Mason two. They were determined to make this shit work.

Dropping him off at home, Mason went straight to work. Bella had been blowing his phone up all night. She didn't believe that he was handling business. So, he didn't bother to answer anymore of her calls. Money over hoes was his motto now.

While he was at work he received a phone call from the Williams. They were going out of town and they wanted to take CJ with them. He let them because he had to make his money. And his mother was taking care of Shantel right now. Rita didn't mind helping him with her.

She knew that he had his hands full with work. She just didn't know what type of work. Mason was her pride and joy. He was supposed to go to college and make her proud. And that never happened.

If she found out that he was in the drug game. It would probably kill her. He had to make sure she never found out. While he was busy stocking the shelves his probation officer marched in. He hated to see his ass coming in the store.

It meant it was time to come off some money. At the end of their talk the man informed him that he was now off supervised probation. But he was on unsupervised for the next five years. He was so happy about that he was gonna celebrate when he got off. He sent Bone a text asking him if he wanted to hit the strip club.

He figured his ass was probable passed out. He couldn't keep his lips off a bottle of henny. His ass was drinking all night while they cooked up the drugs. So, he knew he wasn't receiving a reply anytime soon. He got back to work ready to get off.

While he was working Shabazz came waltzing his corn ball ass in. When he saw Mason, he had a smirk on his face. He really couldn't stand his ass. So, he was going to fuck with his ass. And he knew exactly what to say.

Strolling up on his ass he stopped right in front of him. Mason saw feet in his view and looked up. When his eyes landed on Shabazz a grunt escaped his mouth. He stood up, so they were face to face. If his ass came out his mouth wrong, he was gonna deck his ass.

"How's life working like a fucking slave? He laughed because of the look on his face. He wanted a rise out of his ass. But Mason wasn't about to give him the satisfaction. Shabazz took it up a notch because he wanted his ass to know Rayne was with him.

"Man, Rayne rode the fuck out my dick last night. Talking about a pro Sheesh and that mouth work, my nigga." He laughed turning walking away. He got the facial expression he was looking for.

That mother fucker was asking to get his ass beat. But he couldn't risk getting in trouble behind him. The shit he said got deep under his skin. So, Rayne went back to his ass again. That pissed him off even more.

He washed his hands with her ass. He loved her, but he couldn't handle her running back to that clown repeatedly. His heart couldn't take it anymore. Getting back to work he had a few hours to go. Then he was going to celebrate getting off probation.

Walking in his apartment Mason saw Bella sitting there waiting. He could tell she was pissed off. His ass was going out so, she would be home sulking alone. He went straight to his bedroom and got in the shower. While he was washing his body, she came treading in.

"Where are you going?" She muttered leaning against the counter.

"Bone asked me to step out with him. And he needs to let his hair down. So, I'm going out with him." He retorted not liking her questioning him. She wasn't his mama or his wife. Hell, she was barely his girlfriend.

"So, what am I supposed to do? Because I'm tired of sitting here day in and day out." She whined folding her arms across her chest.

Turning the water off he stepped out the shower. His dick was laying on his thigh as he grabbed his towel. Bella couldn't stop herself from looking at it. His tool was one of the reasons she hadn't left his ass yet. That and she didn't want to go back home.

"Look, I never asked you to stay in the house. You can come and go as you please baby girl." He confirmed drying off.

"Okay nigga. I'm going out then." She sassed walking out the bathroom.

Shaking his head, he laughed at her. She was a big ole baby in his eyes. He wasn't gonna play any games with her tonight. Gliding out the bathroom he went straight to the closet. And Bella sashayed passed him into the bathroom and slammed the door shut.

While he was getting dressed he saw where she had laid out a dress. It was a tiny damn dress to. He knew she was trying to get on his damn nerves. Mason finished getting dressed picked up his wallet and left. He wasn't worried about telling her ass bye neither.

Her ass was being a bitch and he was gonna let her be one. Getting in his whip he turned up the music and drove off. He picked Bone up and he could tell he was already feeling good. Shit he was trying to get on his fucking level. Pulling up at the club they got out and marched inside.

Once inside they ordered drink after drink. The women were shaking their money makers for the paper. But when Rayne came sashaying out the back, Mason got an uneasy feeling in his gut. When her eyes landed on him she came strolling over to his table. Shooing her away he could tell he hurt her feelings.

He wasn't going to pay her for a lap dance. Her ass was washed up in his eyes now. It hurt like hell trying to look at her that way. But he didn't have a choice. This was for the best.

Bone couldn't believe that he treated his precious Rayne that way. He knew that it hurt his boy though. he could see it in his demeanor. Mason was slamming his glass down after he drank his shot. But hell, he wasn't the only one feeling sad and down.

This as the place where he's first laid eyes on Kiana. He didn't even think about that shit before saying he would come. Now being there he wanted to get the fuck out of there. While they both sat there in their feelings, a couple of Shawn's boys came in. That lifted Bone's spirit some though.

He was itching to kill a couple more of them fools. They thought that the two young dudes were all it was gonna be. Well if that's what they thought he had news for them. He sat back and watched them drink and have fun. If only they knew that an animal was on the loose.

One of the dudes got up and strolled to the bathroom. Bone excused himself and went the back way to the bathroom. Going in the guy was using the urinal. He stepped behind his ass then grabbed him by the head.

"Wha... the fuck..." Dude tried to get out before his head was violently forced on the porcelain.

Bone slammed his head repeatedly on the urinal. Urine was getting all on his shoes and shit. But he didn't give a fuck he was killing this clown. Once his brains were all over the place he pulled his body into one of the closed-in stalls. He grabbed some napkins and wrote out of order on it.

Looking around he needed some tape. But there weren't any in there. So, he improvised by using some of the mucus from dude's brain. And that shit actually worked. He got busy cleaning up the mess he made in there.

He had one more to get. And he knew his ass would come looking for his boy sooner or later. And he was gonna be waiting on his ass. After he cleaned up the best he could, he stepped in a stall. If the other guy saw him he would defiantly run back out.

This time he took the time to put his silencer on his gun. He didn't have time to make that mess. Mason would be looking for his ass soon. But he wasn't going anywhere before he killed both men. You weren't allowed to hurt his heart and get away with it.

About 10 minutes later the friend came looking for his homie. Before that some other men came in and out. The friend repeatedly called the dudes name. And when he didn't get a response he started knocking on the stalls. When he turned around to leave he was mumbling some curse words.

And that's when Bone hurried out the stall. The man turned around thinking it was his boy. He never saw it coming. He was hit right between the eyes. As his body hit the floor he felt a form of peace deep in his soul.

He had taken four of Shawn's men. And that still wasn't enough for him. He wanted the rest of his men including him. Stepping across his body he put his gun in the back of his pants. Bone put the body in the same stall with his friend.

Using his shirt to wipe the handles off. He rushed out the bathroom as a couple of men went inside. He hoped that Mason was ready to go. Bone didn't feel comfortable staying around. He didn't know who would put two and two together.

And going to prison for murder wasn't his goal. At least not before he got enough of Shawn's men. He wanted to cripple him and Ant. They crippled him but just in a unique way. It was only fair that he gave them the same treatment.

Mason wasn't at the table when he got back. He looked around for him while taking his seat. He was ready to get the hell up out of there. But he wasn't trying to look all suspect. So, he ordered another drink to help settle his nerves.

When Mason finally made it back to the table, he noticed that Bone looked disheveled. But he wasn't going to mention it.

"Man, this place is lame…are you ready to get up out of here?" Bone asked downing his shot.

"Lame? What are you talking about man? All this ass up in here dude. He retorted glancing around the club. That's when he saw Rayne dancing all up on the clown they beat down. Shaking his head, he turned and looked at Bone. You know what you're right…this place is lame let's go."

The got up and as they made it to the door; some man shouted there were two dead bodies in the bathroom. Mason stopped while Bone went on out the door. Figuring it wasn't any of his business he went on outside. They got in his car and drove off. He kept looking over at his homie.

Something wasn't adding up. First his clothes and how he was so, ready to go. Mason were no rocket scientist, but he wasn't stupid either. Pulling up in front of Bone's crib he deadened the engine. He wanted to know if he had something to do with the dead bodies.

"Bro, I gotta ask…did you have something to do with those dead bodies in the club?" He questioned turning his head to look at Bone. He hoped he didn't lie to him about this.

"Mason, why are you asking me this?" He wondered. He didn't think it was that obvious.

"Because your ass was gone for a long time to the bathroom. First, I thought that maybe you got sick or something. But some dead bodies were found in the bathroom. So, now I'm thinking that you had something to do with it." He explained his questioned.

Laying his head back on the headrest. Bone closed his eyes before he began. He wanted to tell his boy not to worry about it. It didn't have anything to do with him. But thinking about it, he knew he had to give him something.

"Listen man, you don't know what the fuck I'm going through right now. Have you had your wife gunned down at your wedding? That shit has me all the way fucked up dawg. Like I can't even explain how I feel, hell I don't know. All I know is I'm sending her some company. And hopefully I send the right mother fucker with her. I know it's fucked up, but right now that's the only thing that's giving me a little peace. Is knowing she's not alone." Bone confirmed opening the door getting out the car.

Mason sat there a minute watching him walk into his house. He knows he just basically told him the truth. Without coming straight out with it. He just hoped that Bones fit of outrage didn't cause them any problems. They didn't need any beef in the streets right now.

Chapter 8

Bone hadn't realized it had been days since he'd seen Bailey. He'd been drinking and trying to find information. His mother been calling his phone, but he hadn't been able to answer. His heart was broken, and he needed time to himself. He was gonna make time today to check on his baby.

He got on his bike and headed over to his mom's place. She was sitting at the table feeding her grandbaby. She just loved her. Robin loved taking care of Bailey. Since all her kids were grown she had empty nest syndrome.

Stepping in her house he called out her name. She told him that she was in the kitchen. When he rounded the corner, he saw his baby girl. Her big beautiful eyes melted his heart. She was starting to look more like Kiana to him. Robin looked up and smiled at her son.

"Hey baby…you look so tired. Are you not resting?" She bugged frowning up at him.

He hated when she asked him stupid ass questions. Of course, he loved his mother, but he didn't want to be bothered. And she didn't seem to understand that. Bone just wanted to spend some time with his daughter. Then go by the ABC store and sit at the trap awhile.

She cooked him some food while he visited with Bailey. She could tell that he wasn't eating. He was getting thin and he was already skinny. Stress was getting the best of her son. And she didn't know how to help him.

After he ate he played with his baby for a few hours. He gave his mother some money for bills and taking care of her granddaughter. He promised that he would be back sooner than later. When he drove off he went to the store and to the trap. Getting twisted was his goal, it helped numb the pain.

*****

Shawn heard about the killing at the strip club. And when he found out it was two more of his workers, he became livid. One of the dancers pulled him to the side. She said that she had some information. And he was down to hear anything at the moment.

It was one of the bitches that didn't like Rayne. And she peeped the dude that was with Mason coming out the bathroom. He was looking all wild eyed and deranged to her. She was pretty sure that he was the one that killed Shawn's men. And for some money she would sing like a canary.

He offered her five hundred dollars for the info. She told him her suspicion and he paid and thanked her. He drove out the parking lot spinning wheels. His car was damn near on two wheels. That's how fast he was trying to Ant at the trap.

When he arrived, he hopped out the car, he rushed in the trap. When he saw who he was looking for he pulled him to the back. They discussed the shit and came up with Bone. Shawn knew why his ass was acting like a fucking vigilante. But they didn't have anything to do with Kiana's murder.

But since he started the war going off an assumption. Shawn was going to retaliate. He told Ant to find out everything that he could on his ass. It was time to make him feel even worse. He knew that his ass was wreaking havoc based off his feelings.

So, he guessed it was time to get him even deeper in his feelings. Fuck him and his dead wife is how Shawn was feeling about it. He was tee'd off that Bone thought he was gonna get away with the shit. But he had plans for his ass. He was gonna get him where it hurt.

But first he needed more information. Bone had fucked with the wrong one. And if Mason wants to get involved then so be it. He would take his girl's cousin out if he had to. Pulling up at home he got out the car.

Josiah came running to the door when he walked in. His son was his world and he wasn't gonna let anything happen to him. Tahiti was sitting on the couch smoking her weed. It still tripped him out when he saw her smoking. Hugging his son, he told him to go play.

After he ran off he sat down beside his girl. He kissed her on the lips letting her blow him a shot gun. Shit he was stressed over losing four of his soldiers. Who did Bone think he was messing with? Because he wasn't someone to be fucked with.

He thought motherfuckers knew that shit in the streets. But he guessed his ass must've done slacked off. If that's the case it was time for him to pick it up a notch. Tahiti looked at him as he sat back on the couch. She could see the worry lines in his forehead.

"What's wrong baby? You mad I'm smoking up your weed?" She laughed rubbing his thigh.

"Hell yeah…you seem to love the hell out of that Kush." He snickered reaching for the blunt. She handed it over to him. She got up strolling in the kitchen. Her ass was already hungry. The munchies were getting the best of her ass. She sashayed her thick ass back in the living room. Tahiti had a bowl of cereal. When she sat down Shawn was finishing up the blunt. She didn't care because there were more where that came from. He sat there deep in thought until his phone rang. Sitting up he lifted his phone up seeing it was Ant calling.

He jumped up off the couch as he was answering the phone. Looking back, he sees that she was watching him. He stepped outside to see what Ant had found out. He had found out some valuable information. Rubbing his chin, he told his boy to handle that. What he just ordered made him feel sick on his stomach. That was something that he would normally not do. But he felt that he had to make a statement. He couldn't have punk ass niggas thinking he was soft. Fuck that shit he thought walking back into the house. Tahiti, was coming out the kitchen with a bag of chips.

"Damn baby the way your ass eating you gonna get fat." He laughed knowing that was gonna piss her off. She hated for him to say she was gonna get fat. Her mother was obese, and she used to get picked on about it.

"Shut the fuck up Shawn. So, what if I get fat. What you wouldn't want to fuck a fat bitch? Is that what you're saying nigga?" She argued sitting down in the chair across from his ass. She didn't want to be near him right then. She was liable to sock his ass in the face. He sat there looking at her ass carrying on. Hell, he was just playing with her ass. She was always too damn sensitive to everything he said. Rolling up another blunt he thought about what she said. He didn't give a fuck if she got fat or not.

Shawn wanted her no matter how she ended up. Looking up at her, she was pouting like a little baby. The shit was cute to him though. That's when it hit him that he wouldn't live his life without her. He finished rolling his blunt sat it down and got up. Getting down on one knee he grabbed her hand.

"Tahiti, baby I love you skinny, small, fat, or big. They both giggled. And to prove it baby I want you to marry me, today, right now." He confirmed kissing her on the back of her hand.

"Today, right now? Baby where would we get married right now?" She pleaded grabbing his face with her other hand.

"The courthouse we can go right now. I don't want to wait. We don't need a big wedding to prove our love to each other." He confided smiling at her.

"Alright…let's get married then." She shrilled grabbing him around the neck. She pulled him in for a kiss.

*****

A few days later…

Ant was parked outside of the high school. He had a picture of his target. And when he saw her marching down the sidewalk, he pulled off. His ass didn't give a damn about killing women or children. Shawn normally wouldn't let him do no shit like this.

So, he was going to enjoy this. The girl was very pretty from looking at her picture. But he was seeing that she had the body with it. Shit, he hated he was gonna have to kill her ass. He would've loved to fuck her ass first.

He just followed behind the senior. Her and her two friends were talking and carrying on. As they got further along it ended up being just the girl. Ant already knew that she was gonna be solo. He had been watching her for a couple days.

She was about to cross the street to go home when he stopped in front of her. Rolling the window down he aimed his gun and fired. Her body hit the ground as he sped off. There was no need for to make sure she was dead. He was a great shot and he hit her right in the heart.

Chapter 9

Bone was at the trap when he received the phone call. Robin was yelling and crying in the phone. He could hardly make out what she was saying. But when she said Nicole was dead he ran to his bike. How was his little sister dead? Is the question that raced through his mind.

He was speeding down the road. Darting in and out of traffic. He didn't care about anything but getting to his family. When he pulled up there were people everywhere. He couldn't get closer, so he got off his bike and ran.

The people that knew he was the girls brother moved out the way. Other people he yelled out for them to move. If they didn't he would bust right through the crowd. He had no fucks to give at that moment. When he got to his mother he found her crying and yelling out.

They were zipping his sister's body up in the black bag. Turning his head, he felt his heart drop. He had failed his sister, his family. How was he supposed to deal with that on top of everything else? His younger sister helped him get Robin in the house.

Whoever killed his sister did it right in front of his mother's house. That's something that she would always remember. That was some cruel shit. And it seemed personal to Bone. Who would want to kill an eighteen-year-old girl? But he was gonna find the motherfucker that did. His sister was a good girl headed off to college. But now she was gone just like Kiana. Sitting around with his mother and sister for a while. He asked her if he should take Bailey with him. She didn't want her to go anywhere. So, he went ahead and left her there. He didn't know what to do or where to start. The hurt was real that's all he knew. He stopped and got him two bottles before going home. Going in his house he caught a whiff of perfume. And it smelled like one of Kiana's favorites. He searched around the house looking for her. But she wasn't there. It made him feel like he was going crazy.

*****

Rayne was laying on the floor in a puddle of blood. She had found out she was pregnant earlier that day. When she told Shabazz, he said that it wasn't his. He shoved a hanger in her vagina. She wasn't allowed to have a baby that wasn't his.

Once he caused her to bleed he left her to miscarry. She was in so much pain, but he wasn't gonna take her to the hospital. He didn't care anything about her being in pain. Her ass was pregnant, and he was sure it was Mason's. Rayne weren't even fucking him while she was there. What he didn't know was she was fucking Snow and boss man at the strip club. Hell, he was the one mainly keeping her supplied with her drugs. Snow he was doing the same thing plus he was a great fuck. He would eat her pussy like no other. So, the baby was one of theirs not Shabazz's.

She knew that but what could she do? She knew that she couldn't hide it for long. But she didn't expect him to shove a damn clothes hanger in her pussy. She guessed since they hadn't been fucking he put it together. She didn't think his ass was that smart.

But boy was she wrong. And she was paying for it right then. She tried crawling over to the bed, but she didn't have enough energy. So, she just laid in the floor until the pain subsided a little. And by that time his ass was yelling for her to get Malik.

How was she supposed to get him when she could barely move? She moved around the house like she had just given birth. Trying to fix something to eat for her son. Wasn't nothing to eat in the house but some eggs. So, she scrambled two for him.

Rayne knew she wouldn't be able to keep anything down. And Shabazz hardly ever ate anything. All he wanted was to stay high. She was back in the room when she heard Snow's voice. He must've brought over some good shit.

She heard him asking Shabazz where she was. He called her out and she made her way out the room slowly. Snow noticed how slow she was moving. She had cuts on her face and neck. All the confirmation he needed that that clown beat her up again.

He loved Rayne and he wanted to call Shabazz out on his shenanigans. But she wouldn't let him, she was scared of what he would do to her. He told her that he would protect her. And she still wouldn't let him. So, he played the background being happy with what she gave him.

She eased down on the sofa beside Shabazz. He turned his nose up at her ass. He thought that she was over exaggerating. Her ass couldn't possibly be in that much pain. He wanted to knock her ass back in the floor. They sat around getting high the rest of the day. That night Snow snuck her a new cell phone. The bastard had taken her other phone and threw it away. So, she couldn't get in touch with anyone. She was wanting to see Shantel and Snow got her a phone. She remembered Tahiti's number but not Mason's. Calling her up while Shabazz was passed out. They talked, and she told Rayne that she was married now. Congratulating her they talked a little longer. But before they got off the phone she got his number.

Sending him a text she told him it was her. She waited and waited on a reply. But he never sent one back. Rayne smoked some more crack before laying down. That numbed the pain, but she still cried herself to sleep. The next day Mason woke up. He had passed out on the couch when he got in from the trap. Not wanting to deal with Bella he got comfortable on the sofa. Picking up his phone to look at the time. He saw he had a couple text messages.

He opened it up just as Bella came waltzing through. It was from Rayne and she wanted to see Shantel. Even though he was finished with her. He wouldn't keep her daughter away from her. Sending her text message back he got up off the couch.

Bella followed his ass right to the bathroom. She had just about enough of his dumb ass. The night she went to the club she met her a new thug. He was sexy as hell too; shit she was ready to move on. His name was Ant and they were talking.

When she told him that she didn't have anywhere to live, he didn't offer her a place to stay. So, that's why she was still dealing with Mason's ungrateful ass. She fucked and sucked his ass when he wanted it. And he was still coming in all hours of the night. He was washing his face and brushing his teeth.

"When did you get home last night?" She questioned placing her hand on her hip.

"I was handling business like I told you several times last night." He retorted drying his mouth off.

"Well why didn't you come to bed?" She quizzed looking him in the eyes.

"Because I was trying to avoid this conversation. But it didn't do any good now did it?" He inquired moving around her. He wanted to wash his ass, but he guessed he would have to at his mother's place. Grabbing him some clothes out the closet, she started questioning him again. He didn't bother with responding to her ass. Picking up his keys he marched out the door. He was to the point he wouldn't care if she were gone when he got back home. Shit she was way more drama then she was worth.

He should've known that though. Being that she was younger then him. Driving over to his mother's apartment. Him and Rayne texted the whole time. The conversation was mainly about their daughter. Today was his last day of working at the store. He worked a two weeks' notice. That was the least he could do for the man that gave him a chance. She told him that she needed to see her daughter. They made plans for the next day.

Chapter 10

The next day Snow made a point to get Shabazz out the house. He was willing to do anything for her. And Rayne was going to use him to her advantage. He drove them wherever they were going. And that left her the car, so she could sneak off.

She would've used this opportunity to get away again. But she didn't have anywhere to go. He knew where Mason lived now. And she yet to find out how he knew. Pulling up at the park because Snow said he would keep him away from there.

Rayne was beginning to really like Snow. Not for her man, but he was a good person. She still loved her best friend. And nothing or no one seemed to take it away. She got out then got Malik out the back.

They strolled hand in hand down to the picnic area. He had brought them lunch. She wasn't hungry, but she would eat a little. Taking a seat, she sat across from his handsome ass. Shantel saw her and ran up to her giving her a hug.

She just melted from the love she felt from her first born. Sitting on that hard bench was very uncomfortable. She was still in pain from her miscarriage. Something had to be done about Shabazz. Rayne just had to figure out what.

After they ate the kids were on the swings. Mason saw how slow she was moving like she was in pain. The cuts on her face didn't go unnoticed either. He just washed his hands with that situation. He knew he couldn't help her if she didn't want it.

As they moved from the swings to the see saws. He could tell that she had something she wanted to say. He knew they couldn't leave the kids on the see saws. So, he took them to the jungle gym. That was right in front of the benches.

"What's going on with you Rayne?" He quizzed looking at how beautiful she was.

"I want to get away from Shabazz for good." She stated wiping the tear that escaped her moist eye.

Sitting there he wished that he could believe her. But she had left his ass a couple times. And she always run right back to his ass. Mason just sat there and let her talk when she wanted to. He wasn't about to fall for the okie doke again.

"And you will never believe what he told me. And I'm still trying to wrap my mind around it." She said shaking her head.

"Talk to me Rayne, I can't help you if I don't know what it is." He addressed wondering what she could be talking about.

"The day he took me from your apartment…" She started before he cut her off.

"What do you mean took you from my apartment? I thought you went back to him again." He grumbled how did Shabazz know where he lived? That's what he wanted to know.

"Yes, Mason he got in your place somehow. I was playing with Malik when he busted up in the room. I tried to get your girlfriend Bella to help. But he threatened to kill her and me if I yelled. So, I just went with him. When he forced me in the car that was when he told me he killed Kiana." She confirmed crying.

He couldn't believe the shit that he was hearing. So, all this time her ass was kidnapped from his place. Shabazz was a crazy nut case that needed help. Why did she fuck with him was the question? Getting the kids together he told her he had to think things over.

She drove off and followed right behind her. Shaking his head, he felt sick to his stomach. Here Bone was making beef with Shawn and he didn't have shit to do with it. Should he tell him that it was Shabazz? Yes, he wanted his ass dead. But he didn't want his homie to go to prison.

He dropped Shantel off with his mother and drove home. Turning the music off he wanted peace and quiet. Going in his crib Bella was sitting on the sofa. She was texting somebody and when she saw him, she jumped. Mason was so deep in his thoughts he didn't give a fuck.

His mind was on Rayne and only her. All the times he saw her with lumps and bruises on her face. All that shit kept playing in his head. Like a constant replay button were being pushed. Then today seeing her all fucked up just had him seeing red.

*****

Shabazz sat around with Snow watching them clowns. They were fucking with the wrong nigga. His ass was behind everything that they were blaming Shawn for. Stupid assholes, he thought laughing to himself. He wanted to hurt Bone deeply. And he knew that by killing Kiana on their wedding day, would do it.

Yes, he hated to do that to Rayne. But his hate for that nigga outweighed everything else. That fool whooped his ass and left him in a public restroom. And his bitch found him laid out. Talking about embarrassing as hell. He wanted to beat her ass when she said some hard heads helped him to the car. He knew that Rayne's little ass couldn't get him to the car. So, he didn't beat her ass for that. But that shit alone was reason enough to fuck up Bones world. He told Snow that it was time for him to get home. Speeding off they headed to his house to check on Rayne. She had informed Snow about what he told her. So, when he had him park at one of their trap houses, the shit had to be true. He was getting high and talking to himself. Shabazz was getting high on that boy.

That she wasn't to be played with. Snow tried to figure out why he started using that shit. Yes, he got down but with crack and coke. That was as far as he was going with the shit. Hell, he was still making money. He was a functioning crack head.

He dropped him off at home and left. He had some business to handle. But they had plans to link up after he got high and passed out. Strolling into the house he plopped down on the couch. Yelling in the kitchen he told Rayne to bring him a beer. She did as she was told when there was a knock at the door. Mason was tired of seeing Rayne all fucked up. Looking homely and shit. He figured it was time to show up at their crib. Driving down the road he pumped up the music. He was going to get his girl and little Malik. He didn't mind raising another man's child. Since Shabazz showed up at his place he was gonna do the same. Pulling up at their house he parked and got out. He ran up on the porch and banged on the door. Rayne answered the door holding her eye. When she focused her eyes on his face. Mason saw the fear in her eyes.

"What are you doing here?" Rayne questioned in a whispering voice.

"I'm here to get you and Malik."

"Go away Mason I'm not going anywhere with you." She whispered going to close the door.

But he put his foot in the way. She tried to overpower him. But she couldn't Mason had muscles growing on muscles. She didn't want to break his foot. So, she stopped trying to close it.

"Stop Mason, go away."

"I can't do that baby girl."

Then he moved her out the way. And walked into Shabazz damn house. By that time, they heard Shabazz yell out.

"Rayne who's that at the fuckin door?"

Heading towards his voice, Mason rolled up on him. "It's me, motherfucker!"

"Oh, motherfucker you just march your ass into my house?"

"You see me, don't you?"

Standing up Shabazz pulled his gun on Mason. He always knew this day was coming. He knew he was gonna have to kill his ass. And him coming up in his house without permission was the best time to do it. Smiling he walked around the table to be face to face with Mason.

"Ya know I always knew that either you were going to kill me, or I was gonna kill you, nigga. I have been fucking with yo ass for a good minute now. Shit the only reason why I got with this bitch was on some payback shit."

"You think I didn't know that? You're an ole petty ass clown. Who the fuck worried about niggas from high school?"

"ME BITCH! THE FUCK! Your ass clowned me in school. All because I was picking on her, hell what you didn't know is I had a crush on her ass. But you just got your big monkey ass involved."

"A CRUSH ON HER! MAN GET THE FUCK OUTTA HERE WITH THAT SHIT!"

"Well none of that shit matters now though. You know why?"

Shrugging his shoulders Mason looked over at Rayne. She was standing there shaking and shit. He could tell that she scared. He wasn't so he didn't know why she was. Shabazz bitch ass wasn't gonna do shit.

"I got both your bitches strung out on dope and you never figured that out."

"What did you say nigga?"

"Oh, you heard me right. Rayne she was easy she did whatever I told her gullible ass to do. Now Mia… poor little Mia. Her ass couldn't dodge that needle being pushed into her ass. That high was epic trust me I know."

"SON OF A BITCH I WILL KILL YOUR ASS!"

"Trust me there's more my nigga. I was the one that robbed the traps and y'all clowns blamed each other. Now that shit was funny. And yes, I killed Kiana let's put everything out there. Now that bitch deserved it. Hell, she was fucking me, that nigga Shawn and Bone. Her ass didn't know who that damn baby daddy was."

Mason had heard enough. He didn't care that Shabazz had that gun trained on him. He reached out and grabbed the gun. They were tussling all over the damn house. Shabazz was determined not to let him get the gun.

As they fought over the gun it fell on the floor. Shabazz tried to get to it, but Mason wouldn't let him get access to it. He wasn't gonna let Mason beat him again. And he wasn't going to allow him to get Rayne back either. He had waited his damn turn.

He wasn't going to allow Mason to come back and get her. He would kill all three of them first. They tripped over something and they both went down. At first Mason had Shabazz down beating his ass. Rayne then saw Shabazz get in control of the fight.

She ran to the other room. Checking on her son, she opened the door. He was sleeping in his bed. She closed the door then darted off to her room. Running to their closet.

Rayne saw the gun on the floor by the couch. She hurried to pick it up. She held the gun up pointing it at them. She couldn't get a clear shot on him. They were wrestling around punching each other. When Shabazz saw Rayne with the gun. He yelled out for her to kill Mason. Then he tried to turn him around, so she could shoot him. But he wasn't stronger than Mason. And Mason knew what he was up to.

He wasn't about to let this clown kill him. Because he was jealous of him. He wouldn't give his punk ass bragging rights saying he killed him.

"NO! RAYNE SHOT HIS ASS. HE'S THE ONE THAT BEATS ON YOU." Mason bellowed. They were still going back and forth getting on top of the other. Both men were trying to beat the living brains out of each other. Mason didn't want her to kill Shabazz. He just wanted to beat his ass. He wanted his ass hanging on by a tiny thread.

Shabazz punched him in the stomach. Knocking the wind out of Mason. Mason didn't remember him having this much fight. When he whipped his ass back in high school. His ass was no competition, but this time he was.

Shabazz was beating the shit out of him. He was blocking his face when he looked up. Rayne was standing right above them. Holding the gun on Shabazz back. Being pounded in your stomach, was no fucking joke. I barely got out the word.

"NO!"

Then I heard the gun go off. He fell over, I thought he was dead. Pushing him all the way off me. I got up holding my stomach. Coughing and trying to catch my breath. I leaned over his body and checked for a pulse. He had a faint pulse, so he wasn't dead.

"RAYNE CALL AN AMBULANCE!" Mason shouted looking up at her.

She didn't move, as if she was in a trance. He yelled out her name several times. It was as if she wasn't inside of her body. Rayne was there but she couldn't move. She had just killed Shabazz.

Standing there listening to Mason talk on the phone. She was finally able to move. She fell on the floor. Holding herself rocking and crying. She didn't want to kill him.

He was her son's father. She loved him to an extent. But seeing him beating the shit out of Mason. She thought he was going to kill him. And Rayne couldn't have that, she still loved her best friend.

Mason looked over at her sitting on the floor crying. He felt some type a way about her crying over that nigga. He started to think that maybe he made a mistake coming. Maybe she loved that clown, and the ass whippings. Hanging up the phone, he marched over to her.

Swatting down in pain, to talk to her. He placed his hand on her thigh.

"I'm sorry Rayne, I didn't know you really loved that woman beater." He muttered holding on to his stomach.

"What?" She said looking at him.

He repeated what he said to her. Throwing her arms around his neck. Hugging him tight, he pulled her arms from around his neck. He was in his feelings. Thinking that she loved the enemy.

"How could you love him Rayne?" He muttered searching her eyes.

"No, Mason I love you and only you. I always have." She whispered holding her head down.

As they were kissing the police and EMT'S busted through the door. They were yelling for them to get out the way. The cops started asking questions and took them in for questioning. They asked so many things that she couldn't function. She had gotten high and they were tripping her up.

They ended up locking Rayne up for murder. They didn't see why she had to shot at all. The cops could've been called. No shots had to be fired is what their argument was. She was afraid that she was gonna go to prison.

What was gonna happen to her baby? She didn't want him to wound up in the system. She didn't have any family to take care of him. So, she was going to ask Mason if he would. That way he could grow up with his sister.

Mason was released with clear instructions not to leave town. He tried telling them that Shabazz beat on her. But they didn't have any records of abuse on file. He was so mad that they held his girl. Hoping and praying that she beat the charges.

He asked to speak to her before he left. They gave them five minutes and that was all. During that time, she asked him yo take care of Malik for her. Shaking his head up and down. He told her that he was gonna get her a lawyer.

How could they not see that she was abused? The shit was clear as day if you asked him. He couldn't believe they charged her with murder. When he went over there he didn't plan for any of that to happen. Mason was just going to get her out that abusive relationship.

He figured he would have to fuck Shabazz ass up. But he didn't want anyone to die. Not by the hands of his baby mama. That was never supposed to happen. He asked her why she went for the gun.

All she kept saying was she didn't know why. She wasn't gonna let Shabazz hurt him. Lowering his head, he rubbed his eyes. Tears began to form as he thought about them changing places. Why couldn't their lives be normal?

Their five minutes was up. The guard waltzed in and grabbed her by the arm. They escorted her out of the room. She was now in a full-blown sob. She was afraid to be in jail let along prison.

Mason got Malik out the room and took him with him. He pulled up at home and parked the car. They got out the car and waltzed into the apartment. He was at a very low point right then. And he had to change the game up for sure.

He sat down on the couch beside Bella. She was painting her toenails. He told her that they had to talk. Mason got up and took Malik into Shantel's bedroom. He knew that he would have to get a much bigger place, if Rayne was convicted. When he marched back into the living room, she was waiting for him.

"What do you want to talk about?" she asked.

"Well some shit popped off and Rayne might have to do some time."

"And what does that have to do with me?"

"If she gets some time we will have to take care of her son."

"WE!"

"Yes, Bella...are you my girl or not?"

"Where's his father? Why can't he take care of him?"

"He's dead that's why Rayne's locked up."

"Look Mason, I didn't sign up for all of this. I want to be with you, but it's too much going on." she stated standing up.

He sat there looking up at her. He could use her help with Malik, but he wasn't going to beg her to stay. Shit bitches came a dime a dozen. He didn't want her ass anyway. Rayne was the only woman to have his heart.

*****

Bella wasn't feeling the idea of taking care of Rayne's bad ass son. She is only eighteen years old. He is only worried about Rayne's ass. She was all he seemed to care about. She didn't know why he thought she would want to help raise not only two, but three kids that weren't hers.

She wasn't beat for that shit at all. Her ass wasn't about to do one damn thing for them kids. She picked up her cellphone and marched to the bedroom. She sent Ace a text messages to see what he was up to. Bella wanted to get out the house and see him.

Ace: what's up baby

Bella: not a damn thang...trying to see you

Ace: is that right

Bella: yessss

Ace: what you trying to get into tonight

Bella: you

Ace: aight meet me at the spot

Bella: k

She went over to the dresser and pulled out some sexy panties and a bra. The pink ones were her favorite. She knew that they complimented her skin tone. And she planned to go all the way with him tonight. Shit, Mason wasn't handling business, so she was gonna let Ace do it for him.

Bella got in the shower handling her hygiene. When she stepped out Mason was standing there. She didn't even bother to acknowledge his ass. She grabbed her towel and sashayed right on passed him. He followed right behind her.

Mason wanted to know where she was going. He wanted to know if she was leaving him. Hell don't keep it a secret tell him. He stood around and watched her get dressed. She was putting on her panties and bra when he decided to speak.

"Where are you going?"

"I'm going out for a while. I need some time to think about things."

"You need to think about if you want to be with me or not...is that what you're saying?"

"Yes, that's what I'm saying Mason. You have two kids already and trying to take care of one that isn't yours. I don't even want kids. Never have."

Mason didn't know what to say after that. She knew that he had kids when they got together. She wasn't making any sense to him. He got to thinking that maybe she was using him. Bella never asked to move in she just forced her way in.

Bella finished getting ready. She made sure her hair and makeup were on point. As Mason stormed out the room a smile formed on her face. She knew that she was getting under his skin. *Maybe now he will care more about my feelings.*

She heard the chirp on her phone alerting her of a text message. She roamed over to the bed and picked the phone up. She saw that it was her new boo Ant.

Ant: meet me at my place in 20

Bella: on my way

She grabbed her purse and checked her appearance one last time. Bella was happy about how she was looking. She pursed her lips then kissed at herself before walking out the room. She sashayed right passed Mason and went straight out the door. Her ass wanted to laugh. His ass was stuck in the house tonight, while she was getting out.

She paid her uber driver and got out the car. Ant opened the door before she could knock. His ass was anxious to get up in her guts. He loved to fuck young chicks. He liked the pussy tight and fresh.

He liked to get a hold of em before they started going from thug to thug. Ant was shocked when he found out she was Mason's girl. Shawn said to leave him out of it, unless he got involved. But Ant felt that if his partner was fucking with them, so was Mason. His ass wasn't getting a pass.

Ant moved to the side allowing her to come inside. Bella strolled in all happy and shit. She could tell by looking around his pad he was paid. And she wanted a man that could take care of her. She wanted a man that was gonna be all about her.

Bella thought being with Mason she found what she was looking for. But she quickly found out that she wasn't cut out to be the other woman. He might've not been in a relationship with Rayne, his heart was.

*****

Mason was sitting on the couch watching cartoons with Malik. He was pissed off that Bella just left. She was a selfish person and it pissed him off. Somebody had to take care of the little boy. And he was the only family that Rayne had now.

And he was going to be there for her. He didn't care what people thought or said. Mason gathered up Malik and they headed out. He was going over to his mother's house to get Shantel. Hell, he might as well get her, so they can keep each other company.

Mason pulled up at Rita's apartment. He got out and helped Malik get out. They strolled into her crib and Shantel ran up and hugged her daddy's leg. She was so excited to see him. He picked her up and went to find his mom.

Rita was in the kitchen cooking dinner. She heard her grandbaby talking Mason's head off. She turned around while wiping her hands on a towel.

"Hey baby…what are you doing here?" she asked, then she looked down and saw the little handsome fella with him. Rita knew that he was Rayne's son. She just didn't know why Mason had him.

"Hey ma...I came to get Shantel."

"That's good because she has been asking about you. But why do you have Rayne's kid?"

"Shantel take your little brother in the other room please."

He waited on them to leave the kitchen before he told his mother about Rayne. She shook her head as she took a seat at the table.

"Now Mason, you know you're gonna have your hands full raising three kids. It's going to be a long hard road ahead. Are you ready to be a single father?"

"Mom I know it's gonna be a task. I just want to know if I can count on you to help me?"

"Baby you know you can always count on me. I'm your mother and I have your back 100%."

"That's what I know." Mason moved around the table and kissed his mom on the cheek.

Chapter 11

Rayne couldn't believe that they locked her up. She thought she was doing the right thing. She hated Shabazz, but she didn't want to kill him. He was her son's father. She couldn't believe that Kiana was sleeping with him.

She had always thought they had something going on. His ass was too worried about where she was. Rayne didn't care about his ass. It was the fact that her sister did her like that. She was getting very depressed being behind bars.

Her ass hadn't even been in their long. She knew that she didn't belong in a place like this. How did her and Mason switch places? The shit was surreal. They just wanted to be happy at home wherever that is with her kids.

She was ready to kick her drug habit now. It was time to get her life together. She had her children to think about. Rayne climbed on her bunk and cried herself to sleep.

Two months later...

Mason was sitting in the court room. They were waiting for Rayne's trail to begin. Days of testifying on her behalf. The jury came back with a guilty verdict. Soon as the jury said guilty he glanced over at Rayne.

She busted out into tears. He lowered his head; he couldn't believe they just overlooked the pictures of the bruises. She had them everywhere. But because she didn't report it, it was labeled he say she say. Shabazz was dead he couldn't tell his side of the story.

The sentencing date was set, and court was adjourned. Mason stayed around to see Rayne. He was deeply hurt, and his heart was heavy. The high- priced lawyer he was paying for her told him that he could see her now. He marched into the room and saw her sitting cuffed at the table.

He grabbed her face lovingly and kissed her on the lips. She was in tears and the sight of her in pain pulled at his heart strings. He loved this woman with all his heart. He wished that he could change places with her. Mason could pull the time; he didn't know if Rayne could.

The guard said no touching so, he let her go. Mason took a seat across from her at the table. She had her hands propped up on the table. They were shaking uncontrollably. He wanted to hold her, but he couldn't.

"Mason, the lawyer is trying to get me to take a plea deal." She muttered wiping her eyes with the back of her hand.

"What's the deal?"

"Three to five years, I can get out in three with good behavior." She cried looking down at the table.

"No, don't take that deal."

"The lawyer told me that it's best that I take it. He said if we go to sentencing, that I would get ten to fifteen. I can't do that kind of time Mason. I miss MALIK so bad now, I don't want to miss out on his life."

Mason didn't know what to say. He was beside himself with grief. Here he just got out of hell. And now the woman that he loved was going in. Rayne cried the whole visit.

He told her to take the time to get off the drugs. He was gonna be there for her and take care of Malik. She didn't have to worry about her son. Rayne needed to worry about surviving prison and that's all. As the time came to an end, Mason asked her to marry him.

He didn't know why he asked. It just came to him that he never wanted to let her go. Her ass wasn't getting away from him this time. His heart couldn't handle her getting away. What happened last time wasn't happening this time.

She thought that he was being silly. But when he told her that he was serious, she cried again. Rayne shook her head yes then leaned over the table and kissed him. The guard shouting no touching again. Mason pulled away because he didn't want to get her in trouble.

He wrote his number down and slid it over to her. She was to call him every day several times a day. He wasn't worried about the bill. Hell, him and Bone was making good money. The guard announced that visiting hour was over.

Mason stood up as well as Rayne. Neither one was ready for the other to leave. He watched the tears roll down her face. Lord knows he didn't want to leave her there. He stood there as they walked her out the room.

He left the courthouse heading back to his mothers. She had all three of the kids. Mason knew that he'd better get straight back. He thought about marrying Rayne and a smiled formed on his face. But when he thought about telling his mom, it faded away.

He parked his car and sat there for a minute. How was he gonna keep the traps running and be a father? Mason didn't know what he was gonna do. But he knew he couldn't leave the drug game. That was his only source of income now.

Mason needed that money now. As he sat there his cellphone began to ring. It was Bone he hurried up and answered his call. He hadn't heard from him in a few days. And he wanted to let him know what was going on.

When he answered he couldn't get a word in. Bone was carrying on about someone killing his sister. Mason couldn't believe what he was hearing. He cranked his car back up and hit the road. He was going to catch up with his home boy in his time of need.

*****

Bone was going insane. The shit was crazy, and his sister didn't deserve to be killed. How somebody gonna just shot her down. He hoped they didn't think that nothing was gonna come from it. His ass was already on some vigilante type shit anyway.

The fuck them niggas thought. Bone was about to paint the town red. His ass wasn't with the shit's. He wanted blood shed from those that wronged him. And he intended to get it by any means necessary.

He called Mason because he wanted him to know what was going on. So, he wouldn't be questioning his motives behind what he was doing. He knew that Mason couldn't have known what was happening. Because they hadn't linked up in a while. And he didn't want any company while he was out killing motherfuckers.

But Mason insisted that he wait on him to arrive. He was gonna wait on him. But he already knew that Mason wasn't gonna be down for what he was about to do. But he couldn't stop him that's all he knew. His plan was already mapped out.

Mason pulled in the driveway and parked. He jumped out the car and stormed over to Bone. When he stepped up he handed Mason the blunt he was smoking on. They stood there and smoked. When they finished Mason said what he had to say.

"Look bro, I know I don't know how you're feeling, but you need to sit back and think about what you're probably gonna do no matter what I say."

"Right, you don't know how I feel at all. I've lost my wife and now one of my sisters. And you think I should sit and think about what I'm gonna do. No, it's time to fuck everybody and they mama the fuck up. That's what I'm going to do."

"Bone, you can't keep causing us beef in these streets. I didn't even tell you about Shabazz. He was the one that killed Kiana."

"How do you know that?"

"That motherfucker admitted it right to my face."

"I'M GONNA DEAD THAT CLOWN! WHERE DOES HE, REST HIS HEAD?" He shouted pacing the ground.

"CALM DOWN BONE!"

"CALM DOWN… I'M GOING TO KILL THAT MOTHERFUCKER!"

"YOU CAN'T KILL HIM!"

"WHY THE FUCK NOT? HE KILLED KIANA SO, HIS ASS GOTS TO GO!"

"HE'S ALREADY DEAD!"

Bone stopped pacing and looked up at Mason. He didn't even ask the question. Mason could see that he was waiting on him to spill it.

"Rayne killed him."

"Wha, what…Rayne killed him?"

Mason told him everything that happened. And Bone couldn't believe that she finally killed that bastard. He just knew that it was Shawn's people that did it. Here he was out killing his men for no reason. Now he was thinking Shabazz possibly killed his sister.

They talked a little while longer. After Mason noticed the change in his demeanor he knew he could leave. Bone marched back inside his mama's house. He decided to stay with her that night. The next morning when he woke up he heard his mother in the kitchen.

He got off the bed and grabbed his pants off the floor. He pulled them up then walked to the kitchen. Angela was sitting at the table in tears. Bone shook his head when everything hit him like a ton of bricks. He was hoping that it was all a nightmare.

Breaking news flashed across the TV. And that got both of their attention. They talked about the murder of his sister like they wanted to hear that again. But when they said they had a break in the case; Bone grabbed the remote and turned the volume up. A teacher at the school came forth with information.

Bone stood there and listened to everything that they said. They didn't say her name or anything. But they showed a clip of the vehicle that was spotted at the school. The car belonged to an Anthony Sharp. Bone turned and ran out the door. Angela screamed out his name, but he didn't look back.

Chapter 12

"Oh shit, yesssss baby right there."

Bella was enjoying Ant's sex game. He was putting it on her ass. They had been fucking around for a couple months now. She had left Mason and moved in with her friend. She wasn't down to raise any kids that wasn't hers.

He pushed her legs up over her head. Ant was banging the fuck out of her pussy. And she was loving it. After he nutted in her he got up. He strolled into the bathroom and hopped in the shower.

She hated that about him. He would just get his and hop up to leave. Bella turned on the TV and it was on the news. They were flashing a car that looked a lot like Ant's car. She turned it up a little more because it was too low.

The name Anthony Sharp was going across the bottom of the screen. They wanted his whereabouts and offering a reward. Bella knew his name was Anthony, but she didn't know his last name. She was getting scared, but she hoped that it wasn't Ant. She got off the bed and picked his pants up off the floor.

She had to see his last name. As she was going through his wallet, she found his license. And sure, and behold his last name was Sharp. She tried to hurry and put his shit away. But Ant came out the bathroom with a towel around his waist.

"Why the fuck is you going through my wallet?"

"Um, I was just trying to see if you were cheating on me. You know how us women are." she lied, putting his wallet back in his pants.

He believed her at first until the TV caught his attention. His name was scrolling across the bottom of the screen. That's when he knew that her ass was lying. She was trying to find his name. They had his car and everything.

Ant moved toward the dresser acting like he hadn't put two and two together. Bella went along with it getting dressed. She didn't worry about washing up. Her ass just wanted away from his crazy deranged ass. If he could kill a high school student, she knew he wouldn't hesitate to murk her ass.

He was looking through his things until he found what he was looking for. He pulled it out then turned around. Bella had her back to him buttoning up her shirt. Ant stalked up behind her and grabbed her around the neck. He squeezed her neck tight enjoying her trying to fight him off.

Ant had intentions of killing her the first night. But her pussy game was fire, and he was going to fuck her until he got tired of her. But the time was now. He couldn't let her leave and call the police. He wasn't going to have any witness around.

He didn't know how they found out it was him. While he was choking Bella, his cellphone was ringing off the hook. Raising his other hand, he brought the knife down and repeatedly stabbed her. Blood was squirting everywhere. He didn't care he was done with this place after that day.

Her body went limp and Ant let her fall to the floor. He darted to the bathroom and cleaned up. Ant went to the closet and found him something to wear. He put all black on trying to keep a low profile. He picked up his cellphone and his keys and ran out the apartment.

He didn't have a choice but to drive the car they were looking for. He looked at his phone and it was Shawn that was calling his phone. Ant called him back. He needed another car, so he could get out of town. If he got caught he would be gone for life if he didn't get the death penalty.

Ant couldn't let them get his fingerprints. They would get him for so many unsolved murders. Shawn told him to get to their meeting place as fast as he could. He had a car waiting as well as a duffle bag full of money. They hung up and Ant was headed to meet him.

He just didn't know that someone was looking for him. He stopped at a convenient store. He was out of cigarettes and blunt rollers. He got out the car and marched inside. Ant purchased his things and got back in his car and drove off.

*****

Bone was rolling around in Kiana's car. He knew he would be easily spotted on his bike. Her car needed gas, so he pulled in at a local store. He used his credit card to fill the tank up. As he was pumping the gas he glanced in the store.

He saw Ant the bastard he was looking for paying the sales clerk. Bone stopped pumping gas and hurried to pull away. He parked down the street and sat and waited. When Ant drove passed him he pulled out behind him. He followed him to the meeting place.

Bone sat and waited on one of them to come back out. It was a good twenty minutes before Ant pulled out in a different car. So, he drove off behind him. He knew his ass was trying to skip town. Bone sat back and rode the road right with him.

A few hours later Ant pulled in at a hotel. Bone let him get the room and everything. He watched him go in a room carrying a big duffle bag. He made sure his gun was loaded then he put the silencer on. He pulled his hood over his head and ran to the door.

Bone knocked on the door and disguised his voice. He said that he was housekeeping. Ant didn't think anything of it. He moved the bag and went to open the door. When he opened the door, he was face to face with Bone's gun.

Ant knew Bone and he knew why his ass was there. He hated he didn't grab his gun. He backed away from the door hoping he could get to his weapon. But Bone was no fool. He told him to stop where he was.

"You know that you got the gun pointed at me, you better use that motherfucker."

"Bitch I know the rules. And trust me, I wouldn't pull it if I wasn't gonna use it."

Ant knew that his time had expired. Hell, he lived by the gun. He knew that he would one day die by the gun.

"WELL MOTHERFUCKER DO WHAT YOU CAME HERE TO DO!"

"This is for my sister you sick twisted fuck!"

Bone let off round after round. His ass wouldn't be able to have an open casket that's for sure. When Ant's body hit the floor, he walked over and kick him as hard as he could. He really wanted to beat his ass first. But he didn't fuck around when he went to kill somebody.

He couldn't risk shit turning in their favor. Bone backed away from the body. He used his shirt to open and close the door. The police weren't gonna find his fingerprints anywhere. He made sure his hoodie was over his head.

Bone moved as fast as he could back to the car. First thing first he was getting rid of Kiana's car. He didn't want it because it reminded him too much of her. And he wasn't sure if they had camera's or not.

A few days later...

Rayne took the plea. She was transferred to a prison, two hours away. Mason told her on the telephone calls that he would always be there for her. He didn't care that she didn't get to be there for him. He was going to visit her every week.

And keep money on her books when he could. Rayne knew that Mason taking care of her son was going to be a task itself. Once she accepted the plea she came to grips with doing three years in prison. As the days slowly crept by Rayne thought about her life. She was having some bad days going through withdrawal.

With time she was finally getting it together. She felt better inside and out. Rayne could think clearly for a change. She knew she had to come up with a way to help pass the time. And going back to school was something she thought would be beneficial.

She sat in the classroom thinking about what she wanted to be her major. Then it clicked that she wanted to help kids. Maybe if someone would've been there for her, she wouldn't have traveled the wrong path. Rayne choose to become a social worker. She wanted to help other missed treated children.

Rayne began taking classes and she enjoyed it. She was studying in her cell when the mail was delivered. She was used to getting her weekly letter from Mason. But it was two envelopes. It was something creepy about the other one.

It didn't have a return address or anything. Her name was the only thing on the envelope. She opened it first. She was curious to find out who sent it. Rayne began reading it and immediately became spooked.

Dear Rayne,

I'm sorry that you're in that god-awful place. After everything that you've been through you don't deserve to be there. Everything happens for a reason. Maybe this was the chance you needed to kick that terrible habit. Use this time to work on you. Learn to love Rayne again. Then you can truly love Shantel and Malik. Keep your head up in there. I love you. See you soon.

That shit tripped her out. The letter wasn't signed. Who knew about everything that she'd gone through besides Mason? Whoever, the person is that wrote the letter, had to know her well and knowing that didn't help any. Rayne couldn't wait to call and tell him about the creepy letter.

That shit had her all the way fucked up. When she talked to him he told her not to worry about it. Even though it had him curious as well. But he didn't want her to worry about anything but staying safe. She couldn't wait to see him Saturday.

*****

A few months later…

Bone had been spending more time with Bailey. Between making money and spending time with his daughter he didn't have time for anything else. Her birthday had arrived, and he had his mother put together a big birthday party. She decorated everything with Minnie Mouse. The party was at Chucky Cheese.

Everybody came to help celebrate her day. They were all having an enjoyable time. And then Shawn and his family waltzed in. Mason looked right at Bone. He didn't like them being in the same place.

He just prayed that they keep their distance. Shit he still remember the night at the strip club like it was yesterday. They didn't need any dead bodies popping up at Chucky Cheese. The rest of the party went by smoothly. And Mason was happy about that.

Shawn and Tahiti were having a wonderful time with Josiah. It had been a trying week for Shawn. He'd been trying to get in touch with Ant. Every time he called it went straight to voicemail. And that wasn't like Ant not to answer Shawn's calls.

His ass had to relieve some stress. So, he took his family out. Tahiti couldn't tear her eyes away from the pretty birthday girl. She looked like a little princess running around. And she looked just like Shawn and Josiah.

She tried telling him that the little girl looked like him. And that she had to be his child. But he wasn't trying to hear it. He said that the test proved that he wasn't. That was what he was going by because DNA doesn't lie.

When they got home that evening Tahiti looked through every drawer searching for that paper. Her ass searched high and low. Something just wasn't right. How did Kiana's daughter look like Shawn and Josiah? She finally located the paper.

And when she glanced over it, she could tell that it had been tampered with. *How could they had missed it before?* She ran into the living room where she found both her men playing the Xbox. Tahiti sat down beside Shawn.

"Babe we need to talk."

"About what…you see I'm playing the game with my boy."

"I know that, but y'all can play later. This is important."

Shawn looked at her and he could tell by the look on her face, that it was serious.

"Little man we can finish this game later. Go play in your room so I can talk to your mom."

He patted his son on the head as he ran passed him. Then he turned and gave his full attention to his woman.

"So, what's up ma'?"

She handed him the paper.

"Babe I've already seen this shit."

"Look at it carefully Shawn."

He looked at the paper and anger filled him quickly. Who would've done this? If the little girl was his why would someone change the paper. He had always taken care of his responsibilities.

"WHO THE FUCK CHANGED THIS SHIT?"

"Baby calm down. I don't know, but we need to do something about it."

"OH, I'M GONNA DO SOMETHING ALRIGHT!"

"NO SHAWN! She grabbed him by the arm stopping him from getting up. We gotta go about this the right way."

"WHY? THEY DIDN'T! I BET THAT SON OF A BITCH KNOWS SHE'S MY DAUGHTER!"

"We don't know that. He could've been duped just like you. That's what we have to find out. I'm gonna call my Mason and have him come over. Is that fine with you?"

Shawn didn't want him in his house. But he wanted to know if Bone knew that he isn't the baby daddy. Because if his ass knew there were gonna be consequences and repercussions. He sat there fuming while Tahiti talked Mason into coming over. He never had a problem with her cousin, but he seemed to have picked the side he was on.

Mason showed up 30 minutes later. And Shawn went straight in with the questions. He couldn't answer the questions for them. He wasn't around when the test results came in. All Mason knew was Bone really thought he was Bailey's father.

Shawn now knew his daughter's name. He didn't really know what she looked like. All he knew was Tahiti kept saying she looked just like him and Josiah. After Mason left he called his lawyer to get legal advice. His lawyer told him that he was gonna draw up some papers to get another DNA test done.

He told Shawn to sit back and to let him handle it. He was ready for some answers right then. But he was gonna let his lawyer work it out.

Chapter 13

Bone and Mason were meeting up with Dave. They had to keep their men supplied so they could keep the money rolling in. They were sitting outside of the warehouse waiting on him to show up. Mason hadn't told him about his little visit to Tahiti's and Shawn's crib. He knew he had to pick and choose when to tell Bone something like that.

"Bone man I have some crazy shit to tell you."

"What's up?"

"Tahiti called me the other night. And she asked me to come to her house."

"Okay…I know she's your cousin."

"Yeah but let me tell you why she called me over."

"Alright spill it."

"Her and Shawn think that the DNA test results were changed."

"Wha what…what the fuck are they trying to say? Bailey isn't my daughter? Because that's a fuckin lie bro, I saw my test results."

"Listen Bone they showed me the paper. And it does look like someone changed the shit."

"Who the fuck would change the fuckin results? Wait a minute…are they insinuating that Kiana changed the results?"

"They didn't say that. I just wanted you to know before they come at you about it."

Before they could finish that conversation, one of Dave's men opened the door. That was their que that he was there and ready for them. They got out the car and marched inside. Dave had been a blessing to them. If it wasn't for him, they wouldn't be where they were today.

Dave kept them supplied with some of the best drugs you could get. And they met up with him every week. Shit they were making some paper. Mason planned on buying a house for Rayne. They had three children all together and the kids deserved a nice back yard for their things.

Their wedding was set, and they would be married in a week. He couldn't wait to make Rayne his wife. After they finished up with him, they delivered the drugs where they belonged. Then they went their separate ways. Bone stopped and got a bottle of henny on his way home.

He had to have something strong to calm his nerves. Bone was home sulking and drinking while thinking about Kiana. He was about to take a sip when there was a knock at his door. He picked his gun up off the end table. He marched to the door to see who it was.

Bone peeped through the peep hole and saw a man with an envelope. He opened the door with his gun aimed at the man's head.

"Who sent you?"

"WHOA…I'm just here to deliver this." the man said, handing Bone the envelope.

Bone snatched it out his hand then slammed the door closed. He looked through the peep hole to watch the man run away from his house. He ripped the mail open. He read the paper and saw that it was a court order. Shawn wanted them to take a new DNA test.

He balled the paper up and slung it across the room. Bailey was his fuckin daughter. She was all that he had left. They took his wife away from him. And now they wanted to take his baby girl. She had to be his.

Bone didn't know what he was going to do. He figured he was gonna have to go on a killing spree. He was gonna have to take the respect that he deserved. He thought about his DNA results. Bone rushed to the bedroom and pulled the envelope out the nightstand.

He looked the paper over, and he looked at it carefully. When he reached the end all he could do was shake his head. He sat down on the bed and the tears rolled. He was still mourning the love of his life. And now he faced the chance of losing Bailey.

Bone finally broke down. He had been holding everything in. He didn't know how much more he could take. All kinds of thoughts were flowing through his mind. Kiana wanted to get rid of the paper after he had seen it.

Now it made sense. She wanted to get rid of the evidence. He couldn't believe that Kiana would change the results. He told her he would be there for her regardless. She didn't have to lie to him and Shawn about the paternity.

He got up off the bed and got dressed. He was ready to hit the streets and get his mind right. When he sped off on his bike he didn't know that someone was watching him. Bone first went to check on his mom and Bailey. His baby sister Sienna was at school.

He had to make sure that they were straight before he started his day. He hit up the traps making sure everything was good. What Bone didn't know is someone was in his house while he was away. As the day went on he went back to his mother's. He had to tell her about the letter and that Bailey might not be his child.

Angela was beside herself when he told her the news. She loved that little girl. She was her granddaughter. She had to talk Bone into going to take the test. He listened to his mother so long that when he left he had to go get him another bottle of Henny.

His nerves were fucked up. He needed something strong to get his shit together. The next morning, he woke up on the couch. The taste of the Henny was still on his breath. Bone crawled off the couch holding his head.

He had a hangover from hell. He made his way to the bathroom. After he finished getting his hygiene straight, he walked out the bathroom into the hallway. He could faintly hear his cellphone ringing in the distance. His head was hurting from all the alcohol he consumed the night before.

Bone didn't know where his damn cellphone was. But he figured it was in the living room. He had to hunt all around for his phone. He looked between the cushions, under the couch, under the coffee table. He was tired of searching for it, so he used his land line and called it.

He repeatedly called his cellphone until he found it in the kitchen. He found it lying on the rug in front of the sink. Hell, he didn't even remember going in the kitchen last night. When he answered the phone, it was his mother. She was telling him it was time to go take the test.

Bone didn't want to think about that right then. But his mother wouldn't stop until he said he was on his way. They got off the phone and he went to get dressed. When he stepped in his bedroom he could've sworn he was smelling Kiana's perfume. And smelling her in their home was really fucking with his mental.

He got dressed and went out the door. Bone drove his red BMW to pick up his mom and Bailey. They arrived at the lawyer's office and he had someone there to do the test. The lawyer informed him that Shawn had already taken the test. The woman swabbed his and Bailey's mouth.

She told him that the results would come to the office within two days. They would call him and Shawn when they arrive. Bone took his mom back home. He kept his daughter and took her to the park. He wanted to spend some time alone with

Two days later...

The results were back, and they all were waiting. The lawyer walked in his office with the envelopes. He stood in front of them and opened Bone's results first. When he said that he was not her father, he put his head in his hands. Angela busted out in tears and left the office.

Bone wanted to go after her, but he couldn't move. He needed to hear Shawn's results. The lawyer read his and told his results. When he said that Shawn was Bailey's father Bone wanted to leave the room. Tahiti asked what did this mean?

He told them that being that the biological mother was deceased, that it was up to the biological father what he wanted to do with the child. Bone didn't like the sound of that.

"So, you're saying that I have no rights to my daughter at all?" Bone questioned.

"SHE'S NOT YO DAUGHTER!" Shawn yelled.

They started having words until the lawyer broke in.

"Unfortunately, the only person that have rights to Bailey is her father…and that's Shawn."

"This is some bullshit." Bone muttered.

Bailey is to be giving to her father within 24 hours. We can do it here or y'all can meet up and handle it yourselves. Shawn said to do it at the office. Bone got up and stormed out the room. Shawn plastered a smile on his face.

He was happy that everything worked out in his favor. Tahiti had mixed feelings about it. She knew that Bailey was Shawn's daughter. But now she was gonna have to raise her. That's when she thought that maybe she should've left well enough alone.

Shawn shook the lawyer's hand before they left his office. They got Josiah and left the building. He dropped the off at home. He had some business to handle. His worker Chris kept paging him 911.

He didn't know what that could be about. Shawn just hoped that someone didn't rob his traps again. When he showed up Chris came running out to his car. Man, they found Ant's body in a hotel. It took Shawn a minute to register what he was saying.

His wife Candy said the police showed up at their home. He couldn't believe that his best friend was dead. Ant was his main man and the only person that he trusted in the game. Shawn called Candy and she had just pulled up at Ant's bachelor pad. She was there to clean it up, so she could sell it.

Candy had been wanting out her marriage to Ant. He wasn't shit and he cheated all the time. She knew that he killed people for Shawn. And she wasn't into that lifestyle. If it wasn't for the money that he gave her she would've been gone.

She was gonna sell everything get the money and bounce. Candy was going back home to her family. But this time when she arrived she would be a very rich woman. She strolled through the house checking everything out. She walked into the bedroom and there laid a dead body.

Candy screamed out and rushed back to her purse. She searched for her cellphone. When she located it, she called the police and told them about the dead body and where she was. Candy stepped outside to smoke a cigarette and wait on the police to show up. Her nerves were getting bad fooling with Ant.

She never knew when she was gonna receive a phone call. Someone saying he was killed or in jail. That was the first couple years of their marriage. Then after a while she couldn't wait for the call. Ant wouldn't let her leave his ass, and him being dead was her only way out.

The police showed up and they did what they do. They had the news crew there and everything. Candy wasn't trying to be on television. She just wanted them to get the body out of there. Hell, she was just trying to sell the place.

Chapter 4

Bone was so pissed off. His mother cried the whole way back to her house. They pulled up and got out the car. Angela ran in and picked Bailey up. She hugged her and cried.

He couldn't stand the sight of his mother crying. He knew that she was hurting just as bad as him. Bone didn't know how he was going to give Bailey up. Sienna was sad because she knew what the results were. He took his daughter away from his mother.

Angela didn't want to let her go. But Bone insisted that she go calm down before she upset Bailey. She did and went to her bedroom. He called Mason and had him bring the kids over. He was gonna have her a little family going away party.

Bone gave Sienna some money and told her to go get some things. Mason showed up and he had MJ, Malik and Shantel. All the kids were watching cartoons while they waited on Sienna to get back from the store. The men stepped outside to get high and talk. Mason couldn't believe that Bailey wasn't Bone's daughter.

He knew that he loved her and hated to give her up. Right was right, and she was Shawn's child. He just hated that it was happening to his boy. Sienna pulled up while they were outside. They helped carry the things inside.

Everyone tried to have an enjoyable time. The kids enjoyed themselves. But the adults knew the reason behind the party. While the kids ate cake and ice cream. The men were in the living room watching TV.

Breaking news interrupted the show they were watching. Someone had found a body and the killer's body had been found earlier that day. They talked about finding Ant's body. Then went on to talk about the body they found in his house. When Mason heard Bella's name he damn near fell out the chair.

Why was she fucking around with a killer like Ant? That's what Mason kept thinking. She left him because she couldn't handle raising Malik. He was fine with that. But damn she could've done a hell of a lot better than that.

Mason packed his kids up to leave after the party was over. He gave Bone dap and he didn't see anything in his eyes. His eyes were blank they were empty. No emotion or life whatsoever were in them. He knew deep down that Bone had something to do with Ant's death.

He wasn't gonna ask him. Mason knew that he wouldn't answer him anyway. Him and his crew headed home. They were all falling asleep in the car. He was glad about that he could use some time to himself.

Tomorrow he was finally marrying the woman he loved. Mason couldn't wait to make Rayne his wife. He parked the car then looked in the backseat. All three of them were knocked out. He got out and unlocked the door.

Mason went back and forth carrying the children inside. His apartment was becoming way too small fast. Shantel was in her bed and Malik was on a cot on the floor. MJ was sleeping with him. Mason was gonna buy a house right after he married Rayne.

The next day…

Mason took all the kids to his mother. She wasn't invited to the wedding. So, she was watching all the kids for him. Rita didn't even know that he was marrying Rayne. He was gonna tell her when he got home tomorrow.

The prison she was in had a room for the wedding night. And he was staying all night with his woman. Neither one of them were worried about having a cake and all of that. They just wanted to get married and make love the rest of the day and night. He came prepared with condoms, because she wasn't on birth control.

He wouldn't mind getting Rayne pregnant again. But not while she was locked up. Mason had picked her up a white sundress nothing fancy. He brought her a cheap silver wedding band. He also brought her a very expensive silver wedding set.

Rayne would wear the wedding set tonight while with him. But when she went back to population it will be the cheap 50 -dollar band. The ceremony didn't last long. It was just them two with the guards and the preacher. After the wedding they were escorted to their suite for the evening.

It wasn't anything fancy, but they were just glad to be together. They were happy that it at least had a double bed. The only downside to it was a guard had to stay outside the room. Rayne was gonna have to keep it quiet. Mason had packed them a picnic basket.

The guard had to search through it first, but they approved it. This was the first time Mason had seen a smile on her face. He wanted to keep that smile on her face forever. He leaned over and kissed her on the lips. He couldn't keep his hands or lips off her.

She was so beautiful to him. And now she was all his and only his. Mason laid her back on the bed and mounted her. He couldn't wait to feel her again. It had been so long since he been inside of her.

He wanted to take it slow with her though. He made love to her mouth and her neck before traveling down. Mason began taking her dress off. Rayne's perky breast were standing at attention. He couldn't stop himself from attacking her nipples.

They were chocolate and he loved himself some chocolate. He sucked and licked all over both her tits. She tasted so good he had to sample her honey pot. Mason moved further down her body kissing her legs on the way. He reached her pussy he licked it getting a quick taste.

Rayne moaned out in pleasure as he feasted on her pussy. She was in ecstasy as his mouth made love to her kitty. At one point she had to place her hand over her mouth. She knew that she could be loud during sex with Mason. He was the best lover that she ever had.

He felt her trembling in his arms. And that made him go even harder. He lifted her legs up by her ears and ate that pussy like a watermelon.

"Oh God…oh my…oh shit…"

She creamed all in his mouth. And he lapped up every bit of her juices. Now that he had her good and primed up. Mason climbed up her body and settled between her thighs. He spread her legs open and plunged deep inside her pussy.

"Oh Mason…baby"

Rayne cooed as he moved in and out of her. He was hitting her spot making it sensitive. He kept moving in and out picking up his pace. The faster he moved the louder she was getting. Mason kissed her letting her taste herself.

And that seemed to be the only way to keep her from being too loud. But not only her him as well. She was feeling so damn good he wanted to scream like a little bitch. His ass fucked around and busted in her pussy again. He forgot to put a condom on. And that was the way they spent their night and morning.

*****

Bone took Bailey to the lawyer's office. His mother couldn't do it, so she said her goodbyes at home. He didn't want to hand her over to Shawn, but he didn't have a choice. Tahiti was the one to show up, Shawn wasn't even with her. Bone hugged and kissed Bailey on the cheek before giving her away.

He wanted to fuck some shit up. He rushed out the building before the tears started flowing. Bone went straight to the ABC store and picked up a fifth of 1800. He had to numb the pain and that was the only way he knew how. He went home because he didn't want to be around anyone.

He cracked the seal on the bottle and went in. Bone looked around the house and he had to get out of there. Everywhere he looked he saw Kiana. And if he saw her he thought about Bailey. He had to get out for a little while.

Bone called Mason, but his phone went straight to voicemail. He parked at the strip club and got out. When he stepped inside he saw Shawn sitting at the bar. He went to the bathroom and splashed chilly water on his face. Murder was on his mind and he had to get rid of it.

He was glad that he left his gun at home. Because if he didn't he knew he would fuck around and kill his ass tonight. Bone marched back out the bathroom and found a table. He wished he would've went to a different club. But this one had the better-looking chicks dancing.

Shawn peeped Bone drinking and getting lap dances. Tahiti told him that it seemed to break his heart to let Bailey go. His ass didn't seem to sad to him. He looked like he was having the time of his life. Shawn got up and left the club.

He didn't want to be in the same place as Bone ass. Tahiti wanted him to come home and bond with his daughter. Bailey wasn't warming up to them yet. She would play with Josiah a little, but as far as Tahiti she didn't want her. She cried a lot wanting her daddy and grandma.

Shawn walked in the house and heard her crying. They had fixed up a room real pretty for her. Tahiti thought the frozen theme would be nice. Bailey wouldn't even touch anything in the room. She didn't know them, and she wanted the people she had been around.

"Have she been crying the whole time I been gone?"

"Yes, pretty much. Maybe we should've let him keep her Shawn."

"Hell, no she's my daughter not his. I've already lost a year of her life."

"But she's miserable here with us. All she does is cry."

"She just has to get to know us and she will be fine."

He went to her room and picked her up. She was his baby girl his first daughter. Shawn wasn't about to give her back to Bone. Fuck that clown as nigga. And Tahiti was right, when he looked at her he saw Josiah.

He knew that she was his baby without a doubt. And he loved her already. He just wished that she knew and loved him already. But that was Kiana's fault for fucking with the results. Shawn knew that they just had to be patient with her.

Shawn told Tahiti to go rent some kid movies and told her to stop and pick up some cupcakes. He ordered pizza and wings. They were gonna have a family night. He knew it was kind of like trying to buy her happiness. But if that's what it took to make her happy then that's what he was gonna do.

Bone was at the club trying to keep his mind off Bailey. He just hoped that she was happy with them. Because if he found out that they were mistreating her in any way, they were gonna have to see him. An Asian stripper was rolling around on his dick. She was doing an excellent job, but he wasn't wanting any pussy.

She offered him a blowjob in the back. He took her up on that offer. Bone didn't feel like that was disrespecting Kiana. The girl was slobbering all over his big dick. And he had to admit she was doing the damn thang.

He busted down her throat and paid her for her services. She thought she was gonna get to ride that pole. But he quickly stood up and pulled his pants up. He wasn't blessing any bitch with his dick any time soon. Bone was a sucker for love, and he wasn't ready to travel down that road yet.

*****

Mason hated to leave Rayne in that prison. But they enjoyed each other as much as they could. He looked at the box of condoms and shook his head. They didn't use any of them damn things. He just hoped and prayed that she didn't get pregnant while in prison.

He went to mother's house and went inside. She had all the kids watching cartoons. MJ was crawling around messing with everything in sight. Rita was in the kitchen making peanut butter and jelly sandwiches for lunch. Mason looked down at his ring and smiled.

Walking into the kitchen he took a seat at the table. Rita looked up and smiled at her son. She just loved her baby.

"Hey son, you're back early."

"Yeah… how did the kids do?"

"They were great. That Malik is a well- mannered little boy."

"Yes, he is…ma come sit down I have something to tell you."

Rita could tell from the tone of his voice that it was serious. She finished with the sandwich she was making first. She called Shantel to come get the food. Then she took a seat at the table beside Mason.

"Hey daddy."

"Hey baby girl."

After she left the kitchen Rita asked, "What do you have to tell me?"

"Well ma' I went to the prison yesterday and married Rayne."

"You did what Mason?"

He didn't even respond to her question. He just held up his hand and showed her the ring on his finger.

"Why…why would you marry her Mason? That girl hasn't been anything but trouble for you."

"Because I love her ma' that's why. I always have."

"Oh baby…you got a lot to learn about love. But I guess it's your life, right? I can't tell you what's right and what's wrong anymore."

Rita got up from the table and kissed her son on the cheek. She marched out the kitchen and went to her bedroom. She was disappointed in Mason. He could've talked to her before he made that big mistake. Mason got his kids and left.

Mason got home and got all the kids ready for bed. He was laying in his bed waiting on MJ to knock out. The news came on after the game went off. They showed the clip about Ant and Bella again. Her parents were talking on the news.

That was the first time that he had seen her family. He hated that Bella was killed by that bastard. Mason felt like maybe it was his fault. He wished he'd never got with the naïve little girl. He thought that maybe she would still be alive.

He laid there thinking about Bella while waiting on his wife to call. He just loved that Rayne was his wife. Mason started looking up houses for sale. He didn't like having Malik on a cot on the floor. He was his son and he was gonna have his own room.

*****

The next week...

Bone was getting even more depressed. He concluded that he was gonna get his daughter back. He didn't give a fuck about the test results. Bailey was his daughter and what he had left of Kiana. He loaded his gun before he left his house.

Shawn was at the strip club again. His ass loved to hang out there watching the women shake their ass. Bone didn't go inside he waited on him to come out. He wasn't gonna risk anyone seeing him. A few hours later he came staggering out.

Bone knew that was his chance to take his ass out. He pulled his hood over his head and ran up on Shawn. His ass was drunk and not watching his surroundings. Bone didn't even saw anything he just shot him in the back of his head. The body dropped but Bone wasn't done.

He loaded his body up with bullets. His ass wasn't gonna survive this attack. Bone had been wanting to take Shawn's ass out. He should've never fucked with his daughter. That was the last straw for him.

Bone emptied his clip then hurried back to his car. He drove out the parking lot and headed home. He had to wait for the body to be found before he went to Tahiti. Bone was going to get his baby girl back. He thought about Kiana changing the results.

He knew that she wanted him to be Bailey's father. And he wasn't gonna let Shawn and Tahiti change that. Bone walked in his house with a heavy heart. He went over to Kiana's Urn and picked it up. He hadn't looked at the damn thing since he took it home.

He felt like he needed her more now than he ever did. Bone took it and sat down on the couch. He talked to her for a while. He just wished that she could answer his questions. Because he had a boat load of them for her. Bone drunk all his liquor that he had while talking to her, before passing out.

*****

Tahiti was asleep when there was a knock at the door. She was startled and shaken up. She jumped up and ran to the door. Whoever it was they were knocking like the police. She thought that it was Shawn and he had lost his key.

When she opened the door, it was two policemen standing on her porch. Tahiti was standing there in a tank top without a bra and girl boxers. She felt naked standing there in front of them. She backed up and hide behind the door. Tahiti was wondering why they were there.

"Sorry to bother you ma'am, are you the wife of Shawn Wilson?"

"Yes…is he alright?"

Tahiti asked with worry laced in her voice. She could tell that they came bearing shocking news. What they said next, she wasn't expecting at all.

"We regret to inform you that his body was found in the parking lot of Kevin's strip club."

"NO! no, no…no you have to be talking about somebody else."

They didn't say anything to her little rant. That's when she knew that they were telling her the truth. She fell back crying and screaming out that it couldn't be true. The police officers tried to console her before they started questioning her. One officer helped her to the couch.

The other one went and got her something to drink. When she finally got it together they began asking her questions. They wanted to know if Shawn had any enemy's. Tahiti didn't know if he had any or not. He didn't allow her to be all up in his busy like that.

She still couldn't believe that he was gone. They were finally getting it right. They had a family now and some asshole took that away from them. She answered what she could, then they gave her a card. They said if she remembered anything else to give them a call.

After they left she sat down and cried. She knew that she was gonna have to tell Josiah. Tahiti didn't know how he was going to take it. She didn't know how to tell him the sad news. The news about Shawn had her in a fucked- up place.

She had to pull herself together before she attempted to tell him. She was getting depressed just thinking about telling him about his father. The thought of having two children to raise weighed heavy on her mind as well. Tahiti pulled herself up off the couch and mopped to the bedroom.

She was surprised that she didn't wake the kids up when the police were there. Tahiti was happy that both kids could sleep through a tornado. She laid down on the bed and cried herself to sleep. She slept long as she could. Tahiti hoped to wake up and it was all a dream.

*****

Bone woke up the next morning on the couch. The Urn was sitting on the coffee table beside his empty bottle of Henny. Thoughts of the night before flooded his mind. He hurried and grabbed the remote to turn the TV on. He searched through the channels until he found the news.

He never watched the news, so he didn't know the channel. His cellphone rang, and he looked and saw it was Mason calling. That alone let him know that the news was out. He didn't want to hear what he had to say. Bone sent him to voicemail then turned the volume on the TV up.

Mason wasn't having it though. He kept calling until he answered his phone call. They talked, and Bone acted like it was news to him when Mason said something about Shawn. He wasn't about to admit to killing that nigga over the phone. He wasn't a dummy that's for sure.

Bone waited on them to talk about the murder on the news. They didn't have any leads is what they said. That made his damn day. He got up and put the Urn back on the fireplace. He got dressed and strolled out the house.

He got on his bike and roamed around the town. His ass was in a better mood and feeling good. His mother called his phone crying about missing Bailey. He told her that he missed her to, but hopefully that would change soon. Angela asked him what he meant by that.

Bone just changed the subject. He wasn't about to get into all of that. He went to the traps to check on them. Everything was checking out with them. They were getting low on supplies though.

He called Mason up and told him they needed to handle some business. He knew exactly what he was talking about. He said to give him a little while. He had to call Dave to get a meeting time. Bone hung out at the trap until Mason came and scooped him up.

They traveled the road with the music bumping. Mason didn't want to talk right then. He knew that Bone killed his cousin's husband. He wasn't buying his story that he didn't know anything. The devil was lie and the truth ain't in him.

Dave beat them to the meeting spot. He told them to have a seat. He wanted to talk to them about some things. They handled business and got everything squared away. Then he sat them down and told them he was handing the business over to his nephew.

He told them that everything would still go the same way. All they had to do was hit up the same number and they would receive a meeting time. Same place just a different person will be there to do business. The guys didn't have a problem with anything. Dave said that the changes will happen within the next month.

They left with their work and some doubt. Bone didn't understand why he didn't mention that when they first started doing business. They didn't want to look for a new connect. They were just gonna go with the flow. Bone went straight to cooking up the dope when they got back.

Mason did the cutting and bagging as he brought it out. They had a long night ahead of them. They didn't trust anyone to do this shit for them. Bone said that they were better off doing it their selves. He said they would save money doing it.

They were cooking up enough drugs to keep four traps running. Shit they were making a fucking killing. They delivered to the traps then called it a day. Mason went to look at a house he was thinking about buying. Bone called the lawyer that handled the paternity.

He told the lawyer that he wanted to get Bailey back. The man asked all kinds of questions getting on his nerves. He stopped him and mentioned that Shawn was killed. Bone wanted to know what he could do to get his daughter back. The man informed him that they could start by asking the wife.

That's what he wanted to hear. Her ass shouldn't want to keep her now. She didn't have any ties to her at all. The lawyer contacted Tahiti about Bailey and Shawn's death. He explained to her that Bone had called expressing his concerns about her.

He told her that he was wanting to get her back. Tahiti said that she didn't have time to discuss the matter. She was busy getting her husband's funeral arranged. They got off the phone and she called Mason. She wanted him to go to the funeral with her.

She felt that she needed someone to be there for her and the kids. He agreed that he would go and be there for them. The day of the services was a hard pill to swallow for Tahiti. She was burying the love of her life. Her child's father her soulmate.

The preacher sent him off right. He also spoke on all the violence around. There were a lot of unsolved murders and the community was uneasy. He told them to keep their faith in the lord. He would see them through any and everything.

Josiah was just pitiful. Everyone in attendance felt sorry for the little boy. When the services were over the people gave them their condolences. Mason went back to Tahiti's house to make sure they were alright. She got the kids settled in the room before going back in the living room.

Tahiti gave him the sack of weed and blunt rollers. She needed to get faded. She still couldn't believe that Shawn was gone. He was never coming back. It was still a shock to her system.

The two of them sat around and got high. She started talking and telling him about Bone contacting the lawyer. Tahiti couldn't believe that he wanted Bailey back. Mason asked her if she was going to give her back. She looked at him like he had lost his fuckin mind.

"Why would I give her back to him? He's not her father, Shawn was."

"True, but you're not her mother neither. Bailey knows Bone and his family. She doesn't even know you and Josiah."

"I'm not taking her away from him to. He was excited when we told him she was his sister. That would be a double whammy. And I'm not going to do that to my child."

"I understand all that, but you need to think about that little girl. Bone is all she knows."

"FUCK YOU MASON! YOU'RE JUST TAKING THAT NIGGA'S SIDE BECAUSE HE'S YOUR BEST FRIEND! FUCK BOTH OF Y'ALL! BOTH OF YOU CAN GO TO HELL!"

Mason got up and left her house. He was just trying to get her to do what was best for Bailey. She didn't seem to want to do what was right. He didn't understand why she was being selfish. He was on Bone's side for real when it came to what was right.

*****

Rayne was taking classes to get a degree. She was also going to counseling. Her counselor recommended that she take the substance and sexually abuse classes. She did, and she was growing as a person. Now Rayne knew why she allowed Shabazz to treat her the way that he did.

She was broken inside and looking for love in all the wrong places. She had low self-esteem from the time Jerome took her innocence. Her mother ignoring what was happening to her didn't help at all. Rayne never felt loved during her childhood years. She knew that Mason cared about her as a friend.

Rayne didn't know that he loved her romantically. As an adult she found someone that she thought loved her. Her ass held on to it as if her life depended on it. She didn't know that it was a conspiracy to get back at Mason. Shabazz was a nightmare that she wished she'd never lived.

There was one good thing that came from that fiasco. That was Malik her pride and joy. She wouldn't take anything for him. Rayne had to live and learn and being in prison woke her up. Her ass was wide awake now.

Chapter 15

Bone had been going back and forth with Tahiti. Her ass wouldn't come to any kind of agreement. The shit was pissing him off. He thought about taking her ass out. Then he wouldn't have any problems getting his daughter back.

The lawyer tried his best to get them to come to an agreement. Tahiti was being difficult, and she wasn't budging. They were going to court. Bone was gonna fight for Bailey. He knew that he would have to prove that he was fit to take care of her.

That day he went and got a regular job. He hadn't worked a day in his life other than the streets. He was a security guard at a local business on the weekends. Bone knew that it wasn't much, but it was a start. Mason stepped up and took care of his traps while he worked.

He was gonna help Bone as much as he could. Rita was watching all three of the kids, unless the Williams had MJ. Bone got him a lawyer. He got one of the best around Chris McCoy. His ass was high priced but well worth the dough.

One month later...

Bone was sitting beside his lawyer Chris McCoy. The judge was going over the paperwork. It wasn't looking good for him. The judge said that Tahiti was the primary care giver. And with him not having a better job he thought they might say he wasn't financially able.

He didn't know how to feel about all of that. All he knew was he loved Bailey with all his heart. He didn't have anything to do with tampering the DNA results. Hell, he thought for a year and a half he was her father. Sure, he had his doubts. But she was a part of Kiana and he hoped a part of him.

The judge called a two- hour recess. And Bone just knew that she was gonna give his daughter to Tahiti. He didn't know how he was going to handle that. Waving Mason over they went out for lunch. He parked at a little diner not far from the courthouse.

They marched inside and took a seat. Both men ordered a burger and fries with sweet tea to drink. Bone wanted to be back early and seated. Mason could tell that his boy was stressed out. And he was worried for him.

"I just don't understand why Tahiti wants Bailey. She's not her mother." Bone stated rubbing on his forehead.

"Look bro, no she isn't her mother, but let's keep it real you're not her father either." He replied looking over at him.

"I know all of that, but I raised that little girl like she was mine. Hell, I thought she was mine." He retorted in his feelings.

"Yeah, we all did. I can't believe Kiana fucked with the results." Mason noted.

The mention of her name put Bone in a fucked- up frame of mind. He knows that what Kiana did was some scandalous shit. But he loved her, and she wasn't here to answer to the shit. Regardless of the fact he still wanted Bailey. She was all that he had left of his woman.

They finished eating then headed back to the courthouse. Bone was nervous about what the judge was coming back with. He just couldn't imagine losing Bailey for good. He thought that by killing Shawn, Tahiti would give her back to him. But she showed him differently.

He thought about taking her ass out. But she was his best friend's cousin. And he didn't want to take little Josiah's mother away from him. Marching in they take their seats. Tahiti and her lawyer came waltzing in taking their seats.

She was a little upset with Mason. How was he taking that niggas side over family? She didn't understand that shit. Tahiti felt that she had always had his back. But she was learning now that he didn't have hers.

The judge sashayed in and took her place. She began looking out at the plaintiff and the defended. As she went on about the best interest of the child. The doors of the courtroom flung open. In walks Kiana.

"Nobody is getting my daughter." She confirmed making her way down to the front.

Everyone was in shock. All you heard were ooh's and ahh's as she made her way up front. Bone thought he was seeing things. The thought his eye were playing tricks on him. How was she still alive?

When she laid her eyes on him and smiled. He knew that she was indeed alive. Hopping up out his seat he hurried over to her. Bone felt on her face making sure she was there. His heart was beating damn near out his chest.

He couldn't believe that she was still alive. After all that time and pain and suffering. Her ass was laid up somewhere chilling.

"It's really me baby." She smiled leaning up kissing him on the lips.

"Oh god, it really is you." He muttered kissing her again.

"ORDER IN THE COURT!" The judge chided banging her gavel.

Bone's lawyer called for a brief recession. He needed to find out what was going on. Kiana and Bone followed behind Brian. Once they entered the room he turned and looked at them.

"Bone is this…Kiana?" He implored looking at him.

He didn't know what to say. His ass was still in shock.

"Yes, this is Kiana." He concluded looking down at her.

Brian didn't know what to say. This beat all he'd seen from pass cases. He stood there shaking his head. She was a beautiful woman. He could see why Bone couldn't get over her.

"Okay…um let's have a seat. There are a few questions that I have to ask." He insisted sitting in the chair.

They all took a seat. And as Brian began to say something, Kiana butted in.

"Let me start by explaining my actions. She paused and waited before she started back talking. The day of our wedding was the most beautiful day. I've thought about that day…every day."

"WELL WHY DID YOU LEAVE ME? HUH KIANA?" He shouted banging his fist on the table. Bone was happy that she was back. But the more he looked at her he wanted to know. How could she leave Bailey and Him?

"Baby if you let me explain." She said placing her hand on his fist. Bone sat there and starred in her eyes.

"Bone on our wedding day you made me the happiest woman alive. I mean I was so high nobody could bring me down…so I thought. Kiana continued. And when the shots fired, I felt such a fear deep inside that I've never experienced. And when you pushed me down in my wedding dress I felt a bullet penetrate my chest. I remember I wanted to scream but I couldn't get anything to come out."

"Baby I'm sorry that happened on our wedding day." He declared getting ready to say more. But Kiana held her hand up. She wanted to finish what she had to say. She had to get it off her chest.

"When I got shot on our wedding day. I just knew that I was going to die. The look I saw in your eyes I knew you thought the same thing. I looked up at you and tried to tell you something, you remember that? She asked getting teary eyed.

"Yes, I remember, and I shook my head for you not to." He confirmed wiping the lonely tear that slid from his eye.

"I recall thinking when you did that, I don't have to tell him how much I love him. I showed him every single day. So, he already knows my heart. When I heard the siren's, I thought they might make it in time. I don't remember anything after that but when I woke up in a hospital bed a few days later."

"Wait a minute the doctor came out that night and told me you were dead." Bone emphasized pulling his hand away from her. He was getting pissed all over again.

As Kiana was getting ready to explain, there was a knock at the door. It was an officer letting them know that the recession was over. Bone was upset because he wanted to know why she did it. Brain got up from the table. He hated he couldn't hear the rest of the story.

They strolled back in the courtroom. Everyone was already seated. Mason was seated right behind them. The judge called Brian to the bench. She asked him was the woman the baby's real mother. He told her yes and she let him walk away.

The judge asked Kiana why she abandoned her child. She stood up because she knew that somebody was gonna come for her. She told the courtroom about the cops putting her in protective custody. One of the doctors remembered her from the last time she was there. He concluded someone was trying to kill her.

She didn't know anything about it until she woke up. She couldn't figure out why her husband wasn't around. Kiana wanted to know so she asked one of the nurses. All she told her was it was a reason for it. And the doctor would be in shortly to explain.

When he finally told her, she said that she refused to do that to her husband. And that she couldn't leave her baby girl. The more he explained it to her, the more she started to agree with him. Tears rolled down her cheeks. She hated to leave them, but she didn't want to die either.

The judge could hear the compassion in her voice. Listening to her story she could tell that she didn't want to leave. She felt backed against a corner. And she did what was best. Or at least what she thought was best.

She rewarded Kiana her daughter back. Tahiti didn't care for the decision, but Kiana was Bailey's mother. She got up and walked out the courtroom. Not before she made sure to roll her eyes at Mason and Rayne. She was done with their asses for good.

Court was adjourned. Everyone got up to leave, while Rayne got up and ran over to her sister. Mason stepped up to Bone and gave him dap. He could tell that he was still stressing. He was so young to be so serious.

They all marched out of the courtroom. When they stepped out a social worker was standing there with Bailey. Kiana walked over to her daughter and picked her up. It had been so long since she held her. She just buried her face in the crook of her daughter's neck.

For the first time in a long time Bone smiled at the sight before him. His family was back together again. He took his family home. When they pulled up to the house, Kiana said it was good to be home again. She was happy that she never had to leave. He turned his head and looked at her.

He remembered coming home and thinking he smelled her scent. He just brushed that shit off thinking he was crazy. They got out the car and he got Bailey out. Marching inside the house Kiana flopped down on the couch. She was so happy to be home.

Bone was happy, but he still had questions. He ordered out, so she could spend time with Bailey. For her not to had been around, her daughter still seemed to have missed her. After the food arrived they all sat around and ate. She gave Bailey a bath and put her down for the night.

She was running water in the tub. She was getting ready to take a bubble bath. Bone came roaming in as she was stripping out her clothes. Her ass was still sexy as he could remember. He started taking his clothes off while starring at her the whole time.

Smiling at him she sashayed over to him. His dick was so hard it hurt. Kiana saw how hard his dick was. She leaned up against him flesh to flesh. Rubbing him on the chest she reached up and kissed him on the neck.

He couldn't handle the torture. Lifting her up he sat her on the counter. She was loving his aggressiveness. Bone spread her legs wide enough for him to fit. He rubbed his dick up and down her wet pussy.

She had defiantly been missed. Easing his dick inside of her, he began to move in and out of her with ease. A deep moan escaped from his throat. She felt so damn good to him. He hadn't had any pussy since before she so called died.

He almost nutted soon as he eased inside. Man, how he missed being inside of her walls. He knew that if he went hard he would cum too damn fast.

Angela loved hanging out with her daughter in law. When Bone called her talking about she was alive. She thought he had lost all his marbles. But when she got there she was standing in the living room. They cooked dinner and hung out that day.

She loved how Kiana made her son happy. He was so different with her around. She was his calm in the storm. They spent a lot of time together after that. His sister Sienna loved her as well. Bone felt like everything was finally coming together.

Three years later…

"Malik hurry up, we don't want to be late picking up your mom." Mason shouted upstairs.

Five- year- old, Malik ran down the stairs. He was the spitting image of his mother. He was missing his two front teeth. It was cute when he smiled, he reminded Mason so much of Rayne. Over the years he had started calling Mason daddy.

When he talked to her about it. She said that she didn't have a problem with it. Rayne said that he had raised and taken care of him. That was when Mason became Malik's dad.

"I'm ready." He smiled.

"Alright son, you got your jacket?" He quizzed his son.

Mason was so excited that the day had come. He was going to get the love of his life. They had talked every day on the phone for three years. He drove the two hours every weekend to see her. Malik went most of the time.

Other times Rita would keep him for her son. Spending time with the little boy. Rita had grown to love the boy as her grandson. Getting in the car he told Malik to buckle up. Hitting the road, they sang songs the whole drive.

Pulling up at the prison Mason and Malik got out. They had made welcome back signs the night before. As Rayne was being transferred out the building. Her eyes landed on her man and her son. She smiled, and tears rolled down her face.

Strolling out the gate she ran into his arms. They hugged and kissed until she wanted to see Malik. Bending over she picked up her son and hugged him close. All three of them were smiling from ear to ear. Mason told them to get in the car.

He was ready to get her away from there. Ready to start their lives together finally. They stopped at a restaurant to eat. He brought her a nice dress to put on. She took the bag and roamed into the bathroom to change.

Mason had plans today and he wanted her to feel beautiful. Because she was his life and the apple of his eye. They got a table, both of them were waiting on her return. She came sashaying out looking for them. Rayne took a seat beside Mason and he grabbed her hand.

He took that cheap band off her finger. Then Mason slid the real wedding set on. Rayne couldn't keep her eyes off the extravagant set. She still couldn't believe that she was married. Her and Mason finally had a chance to get it right this time.

He couldn't wait to show her the new house they just moved into. Mason had professionals to decorate the home for them. The house had five bedrooms, living room and den. He had his man cave because the house had a full basement. His ass already had a big 72-inch TV and a pool table in it.

Mason hadn't finished it yet because he made sure the bedroom was to perfection. Rayne's first night home was gonna be one fit for a queen. She kept asking where they were going. She wanted to know where Shantel and MJ were. He told her that his mother had them and they would see her tomorrow.

Rayne didn't know that he had gotten them a brand-new house. They pulled up and parked beside a white Kia Sorento with a big yellow bow on it. That was her first welcome home gift. Rayne got out the car and tears welled up in her eyes. She grabbed Mason around the neck and gave him a juicy kiss.

They finally made it inside the house. Rayne stepped into the house and people yelled surprise. Shantel ran up and gave her a hug. She was getting so big Rayne almost didn't recognize her. She knew who she was because she looked just like Mason. That was the only way she knew that was her child.

When Kiana walked up to her from the back of the crowd. She almost fainted at the sight of her supposedly dead sister. Rayne was at a loss for words. She didn't know how Kiana was alive. Her belly was all big and pregnant and she had one on her hip.

Her and Bone had been getting it in. Bailey was four and getting prettier and prettier each day. Rayne went from person to person hugging everyone. When she got to Rita they both just stood there. Rayne didn't know if she should hug her or slap her.

She knew that she couldn't blame her for everything in her life. She knew that she didn't force her to snort coke. Rita didn't make her become a crack head. All of that was on Rayne's back. She knew that and accepted it.

They didn't hug but they smiled at each other. That was a start. Mason was glad that his mother was being on her best behavior. Bone turned the music up and grabbed his pregnant wife. The rest of the night everybody danced and had a wonderful time.

Two months later...

It was the day Mason and Bone were going to meet with a connect. Bone had an uneasy feeling in his gut. Something was telling him not to go. But they needed to get the money flowing again. He had his family back and it was time to get his money game up.

Getting dressed he watched Kiana playing with Bailey. They had plans to meet with a lawyer the next day. Bone was going to adopt his baby girl. He loved them with all his heart. That morning they found out she was pregnant.

And that was a lot of the reason he was going against his gut. That's something he normally wouldn't do. But with paying a lawyer trying to get his daughter back, had his money low. He wasn't broke, but his money was lower than he liked. Mason blew the horn waiting on him to come out.

Kissing his wife and daughter bye, Bone waltzed out the door. He got in the car and dapped his homeboy. He voiced his concerns about this meeting. Mason heard him loud and clear, but they needed this. 30 minutes later they pulled up at this gated community.

They were buzzed through the gate. Driving around the circled driveway. They were told to park in the back of the big ole house. Bone's stomach started back acting crazy. Something wasn't right about this shit.

He kept his thoughts to himself though. They parked beside another car that was in the back. The car looked very familiar to him, but he couldn't put his finger on it. A worker opened the door and waited on them to come inside. They both strolled inside looking at each other and around the building as they walked through.

The worker took them to a room and told them to have a seat. They did as they were told. Both guys had a weird feeling about the situation. But neither one said anything, but they were both packing. And they wouldn't hesitate to put some hot lead in some asses.

An old man came roaming in walking with a cane. He sat down and introduced himself. His name was Dave and he had everything they wanted. The meeting was going good at least that's what they thought. But he wanted them to work under his nephew.

They didn't have a problem with that. But when Dave stood up and called him in the room, their eyes got wide as fuck. It was Henry the crazy cat from the strip club. Bone knew it was some shit with this connect wanting to meet with them. Dave thought it was hilarious how shocked they looked.

They looked like a deer caught in headlights. Right behind Henry was three big niggas with guns drawn. Bone and Mason knew this was going to be a tricky one to get out of. But they would die putting up a fight that's for sure. They looked at each other because both of them knew it was about to down.

"Wait a minute what the fuck is this shit about yo?" Mason questioned looking from dude to dude with the guns.

Bone couldn't believe Mason asked that. He knew what was up. Henry's punk ass set them up. He knew something wasn't right about this shit. And now they gotta fight their way out of there. Bone rubbed his hand over his face, because he didn't know how this was going to end.

"Oh, Mason come on now. I know you remember ganging my ass. Yeah, I know you do, all over that fine piece of tail. I get it I'm a man to. But y'all didn't have to jump me though." He smirked taking a seat beside his uncle.

"Look man, we were drunk. You can't hold that shit against us." Mason claimed, wishing they would've gone with their instincts.

"You see youngin's these days in time you never know who you're fucking with…" Dave implied before Bone cut him off.

"Man, your nephew was out of pocket. He was messing with my boy's woman." He confirmed putting the shit out there.

Henry smirked looking Bone in the eyes. He didn't like his smug ass. Bone starred back at him his ass. If it was the last thing Bone was going to, he was gonna kill Henry's ass. He wanted him to be the very first one he killed.

"I know my nephew come on a little strong with the ladies. But he would never harm any of them. Y'all should've pulled him aside and told him he was messing with his woman. Both Mason and Bone tried to come to their defense. But Dave held his hand up. Letting them know he didn't want to hear it. It's a little too damn late for excuses. Y'all jumped the wrong nigga this time. Fella's you know what to do, don't get no damn blood on my carpet."

"WAIT A MINUTE...WHAT THE FUCK IS GOING ON?"

Mason shouted getting up out his seat. He grabbed his gun out his pocket and went to shooting. Bone had already grabbed his chopper as well they weren't going out without a fight. And just like he planned to do Bone shot Henry right between the eyes. If they died his ass wouldn't go around bragging about it.

The shit was getting real as the bullets were flying all around. Mason and Bone was holding their own. They wasn't going out without a fight. Them motherfuckers was gonna have to bring it. The room was smoky as hell from all the gun residue.

The shots ceased for a moment Mason figured it was because they couldn't see. Bone signaled him to make a move for the door. They were both out of bullets, hell they weren't expecting this shit to happen. Well Bone kind of felt something wasn't right. He wouldn't never thought it would be to this magnitude.

It was bodies all over the room and both of them grabbed a gun off the floor. Shit, they had to have a weapon. They didn't know what awaited them outside those doors. It could be some more motherfuckers waiting for them. Once the smoke began to clear they could see.

Not one of the men were standing now. Bone or Mason didn't think they had got em all. But apparently, they did, but they had to be certain. They were still very cautious moving around the room. Neither one of them stood up they crawled around.

They made it around the room and checked pulses. Dave was the only one that still had one and it was very faint. Mason stood up and held the gun to his fucking head. He had been pushed to the edge. Those men were trying to take their life from them.

Both of them had families at home waiting for them. If it was up to old Dave, they wouldn't be going back to them. Bone stood up and walked up beside Mason. He told him to kill his motherfucking ass. There was one last shot heard after that putting Dave's lights out.

They scanned the building making sure no one else was there. And when they noticed that the coast was clear Bone looked for the drugs. And lord and behold they were in the trunk of the car they rode in. Bone told Mason to grab the bags and get them away from the building. He went back inside and looked for something to set the place on fire.

Bone started the fire and they both bounced. Mason called Rita to pick them up at the store around the corner. Rita did because she would do anything for her son. She wasn't a big fan of the lifestyle, but Rita was gonna have his back. Mason and Bone got dropped off at his crib.

They took the drugs in his basement and came up with a plan. After totaling up what they was going to make off the drugs, they would be set. Bone and Mason could take care of their families comfortably. And that's all they wanted, so they had their men get rid of the product. Their men were compensated very well for it to.

Mason and Bone went home to be with their families. This was something they weren't sure they would get to do. That terrible ordeal made them cherish and appreciate their family. So, getting out the game was the first thing they did. The money was there to do so, and both of them wanted to be around as well.

A Few days later...

Rayne woke up nauseous and weak. Her period was late, and she had suspected that she might be pregnant. She asked Mason to go get her a pregnancy test. He was all happy and shit. His ass rushed to the store and got the test.

Their kids were getting big now and out the way. He would love to have another little one running around. Shantel had finally come around and she was calling Rayne mom now. Everything was coming together for them. Rayne had become a social worker like she had always wanted.

Mason got home with the test and ran in the bathroom for her to take it. She pushed him out, so she could take it in private. Rayne took the test and waited on the results. The positive sign popped up and she smiled. He started banging on the door wanting to know if she was pregnant or not.

She opened the door and held up the test for Mason to see it. He picked her up off the floor and hugged her. They both were so happy words couldn't express their feelings. After everything that they had been through in life. Hell, they deserved to be happy...finally.

The End!!!